HEARTBREAK Ranch

HEARTBREAK

Ranch

MALENO FAMILY
Book I

REBECCA BRACKEN

gatekeeper press
Columbus, Ohio

Heartbreak Ranch: Maleno Family Book One

Published by Gatekeeper Press
2167 Stringtown Rd, Suite 109
Columbus, OH 43123-2989
www.GatekeeperPress.com

Library of Congress Control Number: 2020940173

ISBN (paperback): 9781662902178
eISBN: 9781662902161

To my beautiful mom, Phyllis, who always believes in my writing potential. Happy 65th birthday, Mom! If not for you, this would never have happened. I strive to improve with each book and make you proud.

CHAPTER *1*

Helena Maleno—Lena as most people called her—wrapped her braid into a bun, picked up a comb, whisked it through her bangs, then sighed at the mirror. Stray wisps of unruly hair always sprang free no matter how neat and tidy she attempted to look. She shrugged, knowing she would never be as model-perfect as her older sisters.

She rose from the small chair of the old, ranch-style house she loved so much. She pulled on a pair of jean shorts and a dark blue eyelet, sleeveless shirt. It was fitted and stopped above her waist. It was one of Lena's favorite outfits.

Under the bay window, she spotted her red, square-toed Justin boots. She pulled one boot on as she heard the old, rickety truck hit a pothole.

Sliding her other boot on, Lena watched, as she did every morning, the Ford pull up the lane toward the driveway. Caught in a daydream, she watched the blue pickup start up the driveway and wondered why people journeyed anywhere else except Pennsylvania for their vacation destination. It was one of the most beautiful places in the world.

Seeing the older model Ford wind through the ninety-degree turns of the pasture fields, laced with white oak trees and red maples, Lena smiled. The truck rounded the corner and her heart fluttered. It was a morning ritual. The truck parked at the barn and Lena's stomach had butterflies.

Eli Miller, although painfully shy, always grinned to himself as he strode out of the vehicle. He knew Helena Maleno watched him every morning, but he pretended not to notice. This game was as much fun for him as it was for Lena.

Eli rolled up the sleeves of his plaid shirt, revealing his tanned triceps while Lena's imagination unfurled. Eli had no idea how mesmerizing he was, which only baited her fantasies.

Continuing his morning ritual, Eli put on his standard Pittsburgh Pirates ball cap, which Lena found revolting. It was worn, faded, and he never went anywhere without it. Today, Eli had his hat on backwards, which usually alluded to one thing.

Hanging in the back of the truck was a black Kevlar apron. Today Eli was playing the part of farrier, which was more than Lena could handle. When he played blacksmith, she could see all his muscles at work. Just the thought of it made Lena's cheeks flush with fire.

After grabbing a handful of blueberries from a bowl on the counter, she began popping them in her mouth one by one. She chuckled to herself as she remembered her mother's voice from years ago. "Lena Joy, really. Put those in a separate bowl and eat like a lady!"

Grabbing a glass from the cabinet, she poured some iced tea and snuck out to the barn. Startled, Lena stopped in her tracks and almost spilled her tea. Eli was bringing her horse, Myrna, up from the stable.

"Morning, ma'am." Eli flashed a smile, revealing perfect teeth and similarly perfect blond, wavy hair that refused to behave under the cap. It was shaved on the bottom but was all in disarray on top.

Exasperated over Eli's manners, she asked, "Eli, aren't you *ever* going to call me Lena?" He never crossed the line.

"My apologies, Ms. Lena."

Lena sighed. "I'll take it. Good morning, Eli! I brought you this." Slowly, she handed him a very full glass of iced tea.

Eli took the tea from her. "Thank you, Ms. Lena! That was real nice of you."

Lena looked at Myrna and Eli. Watching Eli with horses was like watching a master at work. It was like they could just telepathically feel his expectations. Leaning on a barn post, Lena found herself daydreaming again. One of the younger horses whinnied and bucked, awakening Lena from her daydream.

"Carmine seems real skittish today, Ms. Lena." Eli paused with a confused and partly troubled look on his face. Carmine was basically a pretty chill horse. He was still green, but as far as mornings went, Carmine was usually happy-go-lucky.

Lena cleared her throat and stood a little straighter. "Some coyotes got pretty close to the house last night. Derek slept with the Remington in the stables last night. Just in case …" Lena trailed off. She was grateful for good help. If not, it would have been her sleeping in the stables with a gun, warding off coyotes. Even the toughest cowgirls could admit to having fears. Coyotes were on Lena's list of spooks.

"Good help you got there, Ms. Maleno—I mean, Ms. Lena." Eli grinned.

Grinning back, Lena knew how right he was. Mrs. Hopstef had sent Derek when Lena's father died a few months ago, though Lena had to be careful through her gratitude. Derek had developed a very territorial crush and she knew she had to be careful with his heart.

"I sure do, Eli. Now, would you please call me Lena? Just Lena!" Her hand was on her hip, which only accentuated her small, petite build and short height of five-five. It was common knowledge that Lena Maleno was full of fire, and it would not be wise to take her small size for granted.

"Sorry ... Lena. That will take some getting used to, I suppose." He went back to digging out Myrna's hoof.

Lena awkwardly stared as Eli worked for a few moments. Finally, Eli looked up at her standing there, winked, and smiled at her in a way that melted her heart.

Lena heard the screen door slam.

"Eli, I need Zars lunged today. Afterward, please take him out on the new track. Text me his times, please. I'm going to work," Galen Maleno, Lena's older brother, called. Galen never looked up from his phone as he gave Eli orders.

Galen was a hard-nosed lawyer that worked in Pittsburgh. He had dark hair that was slowly becoming a bit salt and pepper. Lena thought he was handsome and debonair. His personality had only changed to all-business recently when their father died. Lena knew he had a lot on his plate. She longed for her brother to return to his old self and often prayed that he would soon.

Unlike Eli's more muscular build, Galen was fit and trim. Lena's daddy knew he was smart, so Galen had grown up learning the business of the Maleno Ranch, not the cowboy way. He was a tall six-one compared to Lena. Always impeccably dressed, he took after their mother. Lena thought her brother had turned all-business because he was not fond of inheriting the family estate when their father died. He refused to give up his practice and opted to work both professions. It was Lena who was now keeping the ranch together. Lena and Galen were close, even amid Galen's recent personality change. They were the most important people in each other's lives. Now that their father had passed, all they had were one another.

"Yes sir, Mr. Maleno. Right away." Eli instantly put an end to his farrier plans for the day.

Galen suddenly looked over at a very irritated Lena, who had an annoyed look on her face and was just getting ready to begin one of her famous rants. When Lena started a rant, no one could get a word in edgewise. Lena decided she would begin this morning by reminding Galen about his heritage. She geared up and started her rant as if she were narrating a special in a documentary.

"Shall I remind you? Lorenzo Maleno's family came to this country and dreamed of this ranch. It was Lorenzo who made it a reality." Galen rolled his eyes and walked away from Lena, who persistently followed him, speaking louder as he looked at his phone.

"The horse ranch started as a trail ride/breeding business and did marginally well. In 2004, when Pennsylvania passed the Racehorse Development and Gaming Act, Lorenzo 'Ren' Maleno took full advantage. Still keeping the family business of trail riding and breeding alive, Lorenzo Maleno built a racetrack on his property and started looking for racehorses.

"It was a plan that was very lucrative for Lorenzo Maleno. He soon began racing his horses all over Pennsylvania, winning millions. He was just about to branch out to other states when his sudden heart attack halted everything."

Stopping and turning swiftly, Lena bumped right into Galen as he looked up from his phone. "Are you quite finished? I wish we had never done that news interview. How do you memorize stuff like that?"

Lena looked at him haughtily. "It's a gift."

Galen looked at his phone as he walked to his car, annoyed that Lena was still following him.

"Lena, don't you have a trail ride this morning? I swear I saw that on the books. One this morning and one this afternoon."

"Yes, I'm ready! Are you keeping track of everything I do?"

Galen just rolled his eyes. "This is a business, Lena. I'm just making sure that there is actual business taking place on this godforsaken farm."

That caused Lena to whirl around in a fury. He turned away from her quickly, before she could speak.

"And, where's Derek? Those stalls aren't going to muck themselves. And Zars needs to be fed."

Lena was turning red by this point. She was not about to allow him to question the workings of this ranch when he was often away. There were nights when he stayed in his fancy apartment in Pittsburgh or his fancy office. She was being judged unfairly and Galen should be more appreciative.

Lena decided she needed to reply coolly and maturely if she was going to win an argument with Galen. "He slept in the stables last night. I let him sleep in. Coyotes."

It was Galen who was infuriated this time.

"Jeez, Lena! For as much as we pay him? Get his ass up and moving!"

It was useless to argue with Galen when he was like this. Throwing up her hands, Lena turned toward the stables when Galen called her back.

"Helena!"

Lena turned around slowly. "Yes, Galen?" she answered in as sweet a voice as she could muster.

Galen just smiled.

"I have two *men* coming for interviews today." Lena noticed he emphasized the word *men*. He had never approved of nineteen-year-old Derek Hopstef. Galen was convinced he should be doing more with his life. "Please try to see if they will work. This place can no longer run on a skeleton crew. Mother is coming tomorrow with the inheritance checks from Daddy's estate. I would like her to see that this place is flourishing if we are keeping it."

Lena suddenly looked up with big doe eyes, not quite sure she heard that correctly. "Wait ... Galen! Did you say ..."

Galen smiled. "Yes, Helena. I told Mother we are keeping the ranch."

Lena could feel her eyes fill with guilty tears, apologetic for every mean thing she had ever said about her brother.

"Oh, Galen!" She jumped into his arms as he twirled her around, laughing.

Catching himself before they both fell, he put her down. "So, making me fall and breaking my back is your way of saying thank you?"

Lena just laughed through her tears. "No, Galen. I'm just ... Oh, Galen! I can't believe you decided to say yes!"

Galen responded, "Well, you know we have to convince Mother, but I will be on your side. Please get more help. Stop turning away ranch hands because they 'aren't good enough.' Do you hear me?" He scolded her, but Lena was too elated to care.

Lena bubbled, "Yes, Galen. I've got it. Ranch hands ... coming your way!" She jumped up and hugged him again.

He kissed his little sister's forehead, got in his red convertible, and drove away. Lena was walking on air.

CHAPTER 2

Lena stomped into the office after a rough trail ride, flustered. She hated spring break. What were college kids doing in the Allegheny Plateau anyway on spring break? Why weren't they in Tahiti?

A sound forced Lena to the window, where she noticed a newer model pickup, driven by a tall man with a very intimidating Stetson hat. She watched as he casually got out of the truck and rearranged his jacket to conceal the revolver on his hip. He was a cross between Sam Elliott and John Wayne, complete with movie-star good looks.

"Howdy. I'm looking for a Ms. Helena Maleno?"

Lena rose from her chair and met the towering man on the porch. The Stetson he wore added to their height difference, shading his face from her. "Uh, you are speaking to Ms. Lena Maleno. What can I do for you?"

One of Lena's favorite pastimes was giving men a hard time. There were numerous interviews Galen set up that had concluded with men standing up and walking out. Lena was a tough woman, and often the sole woman amid a bunch of men. There were to be no questions about who was in charge. Any man that had a hard time with that was free to leave.

John Wayne stretched out his hand. "I'm Dirk. Dirk Catan. Your brother Galen set up an interview for a ranch hand. Sorry I'm a bit late. I got a bit turned around."

Lena stretched out her hand. When Dirk put both hands around Lena's one hand, it was like it was lost somewhere in oblivion. Dirk could snap her in half in a split second, which meant she could not show weakness.

"I see. Dirk Catan …" she said as she pulled her tiny hand out of Dirk's huge hand. Flatly, she looked away and asked, "I presume you have done ranch work before?"

Dirk removed his hat and looked down for a moment. When he looked back up, Lena thought she saw him hold back a tear. She knew she saw an insurmountable amount of pain in those beautiful green eyes, previously hidden before by the Stetson. Dirk was an unbearably good-looking man, with eyes a shade of green she had seen only in a jewelry store.

"Yes, ma'am. Was married once and worked on my father-in-law's ranch. However. Well." It was hard for him to continue. He just looked away from Lena.

Lena could tell that he was obviously still reeling from whatever happened. In another circumstance, she might have found the whole scene amusing. She imagined how it looked to an outsider to witness a huge hunk of a man like Dirk Catan showing such vulnerability in front of such a small woman. However, Dirk's personality and his physical appearance did not add up at all. Dirk seemed to be kind and gentle, not like the solid tower of strength that was before her.

Lena's heart melted into a pile of mush. Although he was huge, Lena's instinct told her that Dirk's heart was even bigger. His long, wavy brown locks framed his face, shielding those kind jade eyes. Something deep within Lena trusted him and told her that Dirk Catan was a good bet.

She tapped her pen on the railing and thought for a moment. "Can you start tomorrow?"

Dirk slowly looked back at Lena, surprise in those jade eyes. He started to smile, and Lena noticed how uniquely beautiful he was.

"Yes, ma'am! Thank you, ma'am!" Suddenly, he took Lena's hand again and began pumping a handshake over and over. "You won't regret this, ma'am. I'm real good, Ms. Maleno!"

Lena just laughed. "Uh, Dirk? Can I please have my hand back?"

Dirk looked down, finally realizing what he was doing. "Oh! Yes. Sorry."

Lena chuckled at this sweet man and his obviously grateful heart. She was amused by the irony of this man's deep voice that was so giddy with excitement.

Dirk rushed off the porch but suddenly stopped on the bottom step as if something had just occurred to him.

He slowly turned, tilted his head up, and looked at Lena with those gorgeous, pleading eyes, Stetson politely in hand. He spoke slowly, obviously searching for words.

"Uh, ma'am?"

"Dirk. Please call me Lena."

Dirk replied. "Okay. Ms. Lena?"

Sighing, Lena thought about cowboy manners and how she would probably never get rid of being "Ms." Lena.

"Gale said something about a ranch-hand house. Normally, I would hate to ask, but I've been sleeping in my truck and the nights are still kind of cold in these parts …"

As he asked, it occurred to Lena that he called her brother "Gale," a term saved only for people that knew him expertly. She decided to keep that in the back of her mind for the next time she came across Galen.

She wondered how Galen and Dirk were friends. Dirk was so open and kind. It was no secret that Galen held his feelings and emotions close to the vest. He was the only boy and a lawyer. He was very intellectual. All these traits made him very closed-off to others. Maybe there was something to Galen that Lena was overlooking.

"Ma'am?" Dirk brought her out of her daydream again.

"Oh, Dirk. I'm so sorry. My mind wandered off."

Dirk just smiled. "That's okay. I do that sometimes."

Lena shouted for Derek. "Let me find Derek for you. He can show you around."

A noticeably young, baby-faced blond kid came running toward them.

As he approached, he slowed his gait. He stood taller and his posture became erect as he approached. Derek looked at Lena territorially. It was noticeably clear that Derek was eyeing up Dirk, wondering if he was friend or foe. Although conversing with Lena, his eyes never left Dirk.

"I'm here, Lena. Something wrong?" The way Derek was eyeing up Dirk sent a message. Lena eyed Derek, noticing that his voice seemed to drop in pitch. Derek wanted Dirk to know that this was his territory and he was not welcome.

Dirk was no stranger to this kind of thing. He knew all too well what young men like Derek were all about. He just chuckled to himself in amusement and shook his head. Derek had a lot to learn.

Lena proceeded cautiously with the introductions, watching the two men closely as she spoke.

"Derek Hopstef, this is Dirk Catan. He's our new ranch hand."

Lena gave Derek a moment to size up Dirk. Looking extremely disappointed in this huge hunk of a ranch hand that was just hired, he reluctantly looked over at Lena, withdrawn and sad.

"Lena, are you letting me go?"

Lena looked stunned. Derek's mind often surprised her. He certainly did not think like anyone else she knew.

"What? No! Of course not, Derek. We are just adding to the already existing help. Galen wants to start racing the horses again, which means that Eli and William are going to be training full-time instead of doing ranch-hand duties. It's time to pick this place up and get it fully functional again."

Derek looked at Dirk and swallowed before he asked the next question. "Who is going to be in charge of the ranch hands, then?"

Lena was very confused. She was not aware that this was something with which ranch hands were concerned, and territorialism among the help was not really something she had the time to worry about.

"What do you mean?"

Dirk let out a little chuckle. "Ms. Lena, if I may?"

Lena waved her hand as a signal for Dirk to proceed.

"Derek, I'm not here to take anything from you, son. I'm just here to help. That's all. I promise."

With that, he held out a hand for Derek to shake as a peace offering. Derek reluctantly and cautiously shook on it.

Lena could see that Dirk Catan was going to be a very wise investment. Eli knew how to handle horses, but it was Dirk who knew how to handle people.

CHAPTER 3

"And just who in the Sam Hill are *you*?"

This was turning out to be quite a day. Lena could hear the ruckus coming from the barn. Eli was already sprinting toward the barn from the pasture. Derek and Dirk were nowhere to be found. Lena quickly locked the office door and ran toward the commotion.

Eli reached the situation first. Lena was startled as she heard Eli yell. "Whoa!!!! William ... Put the rifle down ... come on, man. No need to be pointing weapons at strangers now."

William Short was an older man, a few years younger than Lorenzo Maleno had been. William had been with the family forever. He was a bit smaller in stature, around five-ten, and had a terrible temper. He had a big heart but an awfully short fuse. He was old-school. William was very much a shoot-first, ask-later man.

"This man is intruding. Found him looking at Zars and Maribel! What. Are. You. Doing. Here." William's tone was rough and pointed. He meant business. This man needed to come up with a reason very quickly, or Lena and Eli feared, William really was going to start shooting. No one considered William a violent man by nature unless he felt he needed to defend himself or someone he loved.

The young, good-looking Hispanic man was obviously too frantic to think straight and was failing to come up with an answer while a shotgun was pointed at him. He had a dark complexion with black, silky hair that fell to his ears then feathered back to reveal his dark brown eyes. He was extremely nice-looking. He was as tall as William, but much younger and had a much nicer build. "I ... I ..." He was clearly mortified.

William was not about to relent. Lena and Eli knew that the slightest irritation could trigger William. "Well? Spit it out, son."

Lena let out a long sigh. She was tired of William's temper getting them into situations like this. Her dad had always bailed him out of everything, yet always kept him on. He saw something in William that no one else saw.

"William, put the gun down! Now!"

William's terrified victim spoke. "Lena? Lena um ... Oh, the last name is not coming to me ..."

"Maleno," Lena supplied while William looked at her spitefully. It was obvious he did not approve of Lena giving away any information.

"Yes! Lena ... Helena Maleno. Your brother, Galen, sent me. I'm his client's son. He says you're looking for a ranch hand so ..."

Lena's face was almost as red as her hair. "Oh for crying out loud. William, *now* will you put the gun down?"

William, obviously embarrassed, slowly lowered the gun and gave it to Eli, who quickly snatched it away and unloaded it. William walked up to the young man, who defensively stepped away from him. William put his hands up to show him that he meant no harm.

"I'm so sorry, lad. You just can't be too careful these days! See that horse out there? That's 'Thus Spake Zarathustra.' Fastest horse in Pennsylvania! I'm a little jumpy about strangers who just go roaming around."

The young man offered a shaking hand. "Well, I guess I should have introduced myself to someone before I just walked up to ... Thus ..."

William butted in. "We just call him Zars."

The man took a few steps forward and admired the horse. "He is a thing of beauty, that's for sure."

Lena was aghast. Had William just entirely switched moods in ten seconds, forgetting that he had just held this young man at gunpoint? She just scoffed at him as he began showing off their future prize-winning racehorse. She had no words.

She walked up to the gentleman, impressed with him. Had it been her, she would have either been screaming at someone or out the door. "What's your name?"

The man looked at Lena and answered, "Hunter. Hunter Manning."

Lena walked up to him. "Well, Hunter Manning, if you are willing to shake hands with this trigger-happy freak instead of running away, I say you are hired. When can you start?"

Hunter smiled nervously, still not sure what to think of William. "Tomorrow is fine with me. I think I'd like to go home and settle down a bit."

Lena looked daggers at William and drew out her next remark. "I can't blame ya."

William just looked down until a familiar voice cut through everything.

"What in the world is going on in here?"

Lena just sighed in disbelief. She hoped that her mother, Lois Maleno, had not been standing there exceedingly long. Lois and William had never gotten along. She only tolerated him because he had been Lorenzo's best friend. When Lorenzo died, Lois had taken the first opportunity to move to Shadyside, a suburb in Pittsburgh not far from Galen, yet miles away from William.

Lena thought she should test the waters and play the good daughter. "Mother! How nice to see you. I've missed you." She went over and kissed her mother on the cheek.

Lois returned the sentiment. "I've missed you too, dear. However, it seems you have some explaining to do."

It was William that insisted on speaking, even though Lena's eyes pleaded with him to please stop.

"Mrs. Maleno. This was all my fault. A misunderstanding. Please don't—"

Before he could finish his sentence, Lois interrupted as Lena just looked down. "William, when there's a misunderstanding, I can always find you! You are all dismissed early today. I have business with my children. I would like to make them a home-cooked meal and catch up with them." Lois was a fantastic cook, which Lena missed more than anything.

They all looked reluctantly at Lois, then at Lena, who nodded in approval. They recognized Lena as their true boss and mostly just humored Lois. They all began to pack up for the day.

Lois, annoyed that they needed Lena's approval before closing for the day, was compelled to shout one more thing.

"I will be here all week and will be watching *all* of the workings of this ranch!"

Eli cautiously turned around as if he were preparing for battle. Just as he was leaving, he looked at a very sullen Lena, who looked at the red convertible coming up the driveway. "You okay?"

Lena took a deep breath. "Yes, I'll be okay. You know what they say. You can pick your friends ..."

Eli just laughed. He wanted to give Lena a big hug, but he just could not bring himself to cross that line. Instead he gave her an awkward smile as they chatted for a few minutes.

Lena helped him carry some of his things to the truck as yet another truck pulled up the driveway, approaching Lena and Eli.

An older, huskier man with white hair and a beard emerged from the truck. He was slow and cautious as he searched the many people moving about.

Speaking very softly, he approached Lena. "Hello, miss. I'm looking for Eli Miller?"

Eli looked infuriated while Lena looked confused.

"I told you to never come for me here, Mahlon."

Mahlon looked ashamed but proceeded. "I know, Eli. But ... your mother."

Mahlon spoke softly and kindly. Lena tried to imagine why Eli was so bothered by his presence. Mahlon wasn't flashy or debonair like Galen, nor was he impressive like Dirk. He was kind and wise. It was odd to contemplate the reason Eli was so secretive about Mahlon's presence.

Eli's eyes suddenly looked up. He was full of concern. The annoyance he had felt before was replaced by worry. "What about her?"

Mahlon continued with caution and urgency. "She is terribly ill. I have come to tell you."

The sudden look on Eli's face held so much pain. Lena felt compelled to touch his arm as she had never seen so much heartbreak in Eli's face before. Eli awkwardly smiled and gently removed her hand from his arm.

"Please ask if I may visit." Eli's request was almost a whisper.

Lena looked confused. Eli had to ask Mahlon if he could visit his mother? What kind of person was Mahlon, and what did he mean to their family? Formerly, if Lena brought up his family, Eli would politely change the subject.

"May I come to your place in the morning?" Mahlon asked.

Eli gave one nod but did not look Mahlon in the eye. Mahlon silently reported to his truck like he was given an order from an army sergeant and drove away. Lena was totally awed by the entire strange experience.

Lena looked at Eli, confused. "Eli … what was that about?"

Eli looked back at her. "You heard, yes?"

Lena stared at Eli with empathetic eyes, unsure how to proceed. Eli was such a private man, and she knew there was a fine line between caring about him and prying into his life.

"Eli, if you have to miss work tomorrow, I understand. Family first, ya know?" Lena tried to make it sound as bland as possible. This was a slippery slope and she did not want to push unnecessarily.

"I intend to be here," Eli said it with certainty as he proceeded to put his things in the box in his truck.

Lena turned so she was looking directly at him. "It's really okay!" As soon as the phrase came from her lips, she knew she had gone too far. Eli dropped the box of horseshoes in his truck and whipped toward her. He had never made such an aggressive move. Lena had pried, and she could not take it back.

Lena saw a fire burn in Eli's eyes and tears flowed down his face. "Please! Do. Not. Push!"

Eli suddenly began to pace and put his hand through his hair. He furiously walked away from Lena and toward Bunny, the horse he was working. He grabbed Bunny by the halter, said a few calming things to her, and led her back to the barn. William, who had heard everything, tried to take the lead from Eli. William misjudged the situation as Lena had.

"I can finish my work!" Eli looked up to the sky, then to the ground. He closed his eyes for a few moments, obviously trying to regain his composure. There was a lot on Eli's mind, and he struggled to regain control. Lena and William, frozen and not sure what their next move should be, just waited for Eli to do something. They did not want to exacerbate the situation.

"Please. I'm sorry for all of this. I'm not myself. Just … please. Good night."

Lena and William turned to go their respective ways, giving Eli some space.

Lena ran past her bewildered family and directly up to her room to look out the window. There, she could see Eli, the man she was convinced was the love of her life, crying on the steering wheel. Her heart was racing, knowing she could not comfort him, and she could feel the anxiety inside of her well up like a fountain. Helplessness was her least favorite emotion. She felt her own eyes sting with tears as she watched the strongest man she knew in the world unravel right before her very eyes.

She sat there for half an hour as tears flooded her cheeks and cried for this man whose pain she could feel so intensely. Hearing Galen call her from downstairs, she entered the kitchen.

Running to the kitchen window, she heard Eli's truck start, then hit a pothole as it continued down the driveway. Turning around, she flew into Galen's arms and finished crying. Galen did not concern himself with why she was so upset; he just put his arms around his sister, stroked her hair, and comforted her in the middle of the kitchen.

CHAPTER 4

The next morning, Lena woke up out of her normal routine. Without expectations of hearing Eli's truck squeaking up the driveway, she found it futile to leap out of bed in anticipation. Slowly, she stretched her small frame and groggily yawned as she rose out of bed.

Reaching for her incredibly old, blue, ratty robe, she smelled something that made her instantly smile. She ran to her bathroom and showered quickly. After her shower, she pulled on a pair of jeans, a Rolling Stones T-shirt, a pair of red sneakers, and a white ball cap. She had seen many teens walk the malls in such an outfit, but that was no hindrance to Lena. She felt edgy and sexy in these clothes.

Lena ran down the stairs to the aroma of eggs and bacon. Stopping suddenly at the bottom of the stairs, she closed her eyes and sniffed, allowing her childhood memories to flood her mind. Suddenly, Lois was just "Mama" and made breakfast for them every morning. Lena did not want her daydream to end.

"Helena Joy, really! The Rolling Stones and a ball cap! Such a lady!" Lois sounded exasperated as Lena smiled. The daydream in her mind reappeared again as Lois scolded Lena for being a wild tomboy. Lois just shook her head as she put the plate of breakfast on the table and Lena put her face close to the plate to allow the aroma of breakfast to sink into her senses.

"Mama, that smells divine!"

Lois stopped, smiled, and backed away from the table slowly. It was so long since she had heard that term of endearment. When Ren became ill, she had opened a travel business in the city. She'd bought the building and Galen rented from her when he wanted to open his own firm. When Ren had passed away, Lois had moved to Pittsburgh and never looked back. When she had enough saved, she had sold her apartment near the Waterfront to Galen and bought a small house in Shadyside. Her visits to the farmhouse became less frequent and her relationship with her youngest daughter had grown more distant. Being a country girl at heart, Lena avoided the city.

"Well, you better eat up and deal with that tall drink of water waiting for you on the porch." Lois turned around and grinned to herself as Lena dived for the window.

Lena was astonished to find Eli pacing in front of the window. He looked especially beautiful today in dark jeans and a black V-neck T-shirt that clung to him in all the right places, causing Lena to wince just looking at him. "Mama ..." Lena looked at her with pleading eyes as she shoved another piece of bacon quickly in her mouth and shoveled another bite of eggs in.

"Lena, really! You should have been a boy! Go on now. I'll clean this up."

Lena smiled wildly, grabbed two more pieces of bacon, and flew through the door. Lois just shook her head and smiled to herself. "If that girl isn't in love, I'll eat my foot," she mumbled to herself.

"What was that?" Lena looked back. Lois didn't realize that she had said anything.

"Oh!" Waving her off, Lois just walked away. "Nothing, dear. Just talking to myself."

Stopping, Lena turned the doorknob and decided to remove her hand and turn toward her mother. "Mama?"

Lois stopped to look at her youngest daughter, bewildered. "Yes?"

Lena was never one for heartfelt family moments. She was always full of fire. "Um ... well." She found herself stumbling on the words and fiddling with her hands, embarrassingly. This was uncharted territory for Lena, but she felt it was time for her to be a grown-up and honestly display her feelings about something.

"Oh, Lena. Spit it out, my girl!"

Lena sighed and blurted out, "Mama ... I'm really glad you're back." Not exactly what she had imagined, but it was a start. Lena suddenly found herself bounding over the linoleum and into the arms of her mother, who nearly fell over in shock.

When Lena broke free of the very surprising embrace, she could see Lois trying to be inconspicuous about wiping a tear away from her face. She had touched her mother's heart in a way she probably never had before. Smiling as she backed out the door, she decided to just allow that sentiment to effervesce.

Eli stopped his pacing the moment he saw Lena. Although he was a mess, he grinned at how Lena was dressed, clueing him in on her mood for that day. She secretly loved it when he chuckled at her fashion sense, although she pretended to be aghast.

That chuckle was short-lived. Eli looked away from Lena and picked up his pacing routine again. This time, he threaded his hand through his hair, always a sign of stress. He was obviously in a terrible state, and Lena noticed how gorgeous he was when vulnerable.

Lena decided to play it cool. Eli was sometimes like a skittish colt, and she needed to prevent him from running off because she scared him.

"Eli! Fancy finding you on my porch this morning. Is everything okay? Is your mother well?"

Sitting on the picnic bench, he patted the place beside him, motioning for Lena to sit. Lena took her place beside him while taking her hat off and allowing her mahogany hair to tumble down her back. Eli suddenly froze, as if losing his concentration for a moment, causing Lena to grin. Trying to remember she was just Eli's friend, she put in the back of her mind that Eli was obviously mesmerized by her hair. She put her hat on the picnic table behind her, then looked at him.

Eli looked at Lena with those unique turquoise eyes. She had thought for the longest time that he wore contacts. Her theory had been proven wrong when Eli was taken to the hospital once, for welder's flash, proving that his eye color was real.

"Lena, I'm so sorry for how I acted yesterday ..." He was looking right into her soul and she could tell he was very embarrassed. She looked straight back at him and searched for ways in which she could cure every heartache he felt. It was like walking a tightrope. She wanted to ease Eli's feelings while treading lightly so he would not run.

Lena decided to remind him that she understood his pain. Not long ago, she had felt what he felt. She knew how painful it was to hear about the illness of a parent that you believe is going to be invincible forever. Feeling those emotions well up inside of her all over again, tears started to stream down her face.

"Oh, Eli! There is absolutely no apology necessary. You forget that I lost Daddy not that long ago. I completely understand! You were there for me, Eli. You kept everything running when Daddy was sick and passed. We all fell apart, but it was you that kept everything together! I just want to help you! Can you understand that?"

Lena just now noticed that her hand had instinctively moved to Eli's thigh. She didn't do it on purpose. It just ... happened. She battled with whether she should move it or leave it. She decided to just leave it there as the gesture of friendship in which it was intended.

Eli looked away nervously. Lena could tell that the next words were hard for him. "Thank you, Lena. My mother passed last night. I'll be taking this weekend off. If that's still okay?"

With that, he looked up for just an instant with tears beginning to pool in those beautiful eyes. Lena thought her heart would just melt right through her entire body. She tilted her head to the side and looked at him with empathy. These feelings were all too real for her and she remembered them well. Eli looked away, embarrassed of his tears.

"Oh, Eli. Please say there is something else I can do besides just giving you a much-deserved weekend off. Can I bring you supper later? Please, Eli." Lena was pleading with him at this point.

He put his hand on top of hers. "Thank you, Lena. Just the weekend off. That will be a huge help."

Lena put her other hand on top of his. "Then I insist it be a paid weekend off. You are owed a paid weekend off, anyway."

Eli tried to argue. "That's not necessary."

Lena argued right back. "Eli Miller! Haven't you learned that you aren't about to win an argument with me?" Playfully, she grinned at him, hoping that the flirtatious comment would make him smile. He grinned slightly.

Then tears pooled in his eyes again. Eli stood up and put the ball cap back on that Lena hated so much. Lena did something bold that she didn't even expect of herself.

She leaped off the bench and pulled Eli into a big hug. Caught off guard, Eli was not sure what to do, but he relented and hugged her back. At first, it was awkward and rigid, but he eventually gave in and pulled Lena close to him. Lena put her head on his shoulder and rubbed his back. Eli realized that he was out of line and pulled out of the hug quickly.

"I'm … I'm …"

Lena jumped in. "If you say sorry, I'm going to fire you right here on the spot!" Then, she smiled, making Eli blush.

As Eli stood, she realized he was still holding her hand. "Thank you, Lena. You are a good friend. I must be going."

Lena felt that word, "friend," cut like a knife. However, Eli wasn't in a place to discuss anything else. That's what he needed right now. Lena was happy to oblige.

CHAPTER 5

"Dammit, woman! How many times do I have to tell you! That horse will run when he's ready! He can't be pushed! We haven't found the right jockey for him, anyway!"

Lena walked into the barn to find the usual, a nasty fight between William and her mother. In all her years of childhood, she could only remember friction between the two of them. Lois had wanted William fired. Daddy had wanted him to stay. William was good at his job, but he had a very short fuse.

Lena decided not to enter the barn any further. Instinctually, she figured that if she eavesdropped just a bit, she might find out what the bitterness was between these two after all these years. Lena decided to lean on a post near a bale of hay at the entrance to the barn, unseen.

Lois fired right back. "That horse is doing us no good running on this practice track every day!"

Ren Maleno had built a practice track on the grounds of his ranch. People would come and rent time on it for practice before taking their horses to Presque Isle Downs or the Meadows. He'd made quite a bit of money just on renting the track. On occasion, he would run a charity event or two.

William was pacing this time. It was a very frustrating day for the men of Maleno Ranch.

"One of these days, you will have to listen to me, Lois!"

27

Lois stopped by the fence and investigated the stable holding one of the new foals. Lena had to strain to hear what she said next. "Last time I listened to you, William, it almost cost me my marriage."

William was obviously stunned by the comment made by Lois. He wasn't the only one. Lena sat down on the bale of hay, suddenly feeling faint.

After a long moment of silence, she could hear William respond. "Why would you bring that up?"

"I came here to talk about it. Ren's gone, William. She should know."

William cut her off before she could finish, obviously becoming unglued.

"No! You and Lorenzo Maleno raised a fine family, Lois. You know the deal. I got to stay. I saw her grow up. That's all I asked for. That's all I will ever ask for."

Lois moved closer to William. They were just feet away from Lena, even though she was just out of sight, still eavesdropping.

"Ren was gracious to us both. More than he should have been. She's grown up now, Billy. She needs to know."

William's voice turned softer. Lena thought it was more of a whisper. "You haven't called me Billy in so many years."

Suddenly, Lena felt short of breath. Her head was putting facts together. William 'got' to stay? He got to see her grow up. That was all he'd asked for. "She needs to know." Lena knew what it all meant. She wanted to deny it.

She tried to tell herself to calm down but was having difficulty. William Short was her *father*? Her mother had had an affair. Why had her daddy been gracious?

Then, she felt it. The tightness in her chest. *Breathe in ...*
breathe out ... Lena tried to calm herself down, but she knew it
was happening. The wheezing came soon after.

She was having one of her infamous asthma attacks. This
was the only thing she truly despised about her life. Although
she knew better, she had no inhaler on her person. Her wheezing
was causing her to panic and she began to turn blue.

Suddenly, she heard Derek's voice. "Oh my God! Lena!
Help! Someone!" He had just come in from feeding the cows.

Lois and William were already on the run when they heard
the wheezing. Lois sprang into action. "Oh sweet Jesus. Okay.
Derek, run to the house. In my purse is an inhaler. Bring it right
back. Billy, call 911."

William was already on the phone.

Lois turned back to Lena. "Lena ... calm breaths. Lena,
were you listening to William and me? Is that what caused this?
Nice and steady ..."

Suddenly, Lena's eyes filled with tears. She could hear
footsteps as Derek handed her the inhaler.

William put the phone down long enough to tell everyone
that help was on the way.

William moved toward Lena to check on her, but she slapped
his hand away just as an ambulance pulled up. Lois looked at
William with sad eyes. She suddenly realized that Lena had been
listening the entire time. Lois and William had caused this attack.

"What have you done this time, William!" a shouting
Derek suddenly pulled William toward him by the collar of his
flannel shirt. William tried to remain calm but was having an
exceedingly difficult time of it. It was no secret that Derek and
William were not the best of friends.

Fire flared from William's amber eyes. "Kid, I urge you to point that tongue on the other side of your face. I mean that with every kindness I can possibly muster at this moment."

Lois followed Lena into the ambulance. As the doors shut, Lois promised to keep William updated.

Derek was not convinced that he needed to leave this situation alone.

"You wanna make something of it? Go ahead! I'm ready!" Reluctantly, he shoved William. It was obvious that he was nervous about fighting William, who might not be as tall as the other ranch hands but was just as solid. With his experience, it was plausible that William could clean up in a fight between himself and Derek.

Derek pulled up his fists, certain that the short-fused older man would take a swing. He planted his feet, ready for an encounter.

As if sent in on cue during an off-Broadway production, Dirk strode in from lunging Zars. "Whoa there, young stud! I think you ought to put those guns away."

Derek was not amused by Dirk commenting on his arms as 'guns.' This fueled a fire in Derek that suddenly started to spread out of control.

"I'm not that young! And, I'm defending Lena's honor!"

Both men looked at each other, realizing that Derek had never been in a fight before. Derek began to jump around both men, poking fists, but not making contact. He jumped on his toes from one foot to the other, obviously his way of being ready for one of them to make the first move. Neither gentleman wanted to be the one to go down in history as Derek's first punch. William and Derek watched this display for a few seconds, then calmly looked at each other.

William decided to try to reason with him first. "Derek, you are gonna get your heart all twisted up, son. Put your heart away along with that temper."

Dirk decided to add his two cents. "Yeah, kid. You're a good boy. You should be out chasing girls your own age and getting into trouble. Not pining away here at a broken-down ranch in Podunk, USA."

Derek put down his arms, straightened his back, and stepped up to the two gentlemen, speaking very slowly but very pointedly. It was almost eerie how calm and serious he became and how fast his mood changed.

"I am not young. You will both see. If it weren't for me, Lena wouldn't have survived a lot of what she's been through the past three months. Including today. She *needs* me." He drew out the word "needs" and spoke in a lower voice than usual.

Both men just stared at Derek, feeling very uneasy about the very creepy nature he was displaying. Derek suddenly turned to Dirk.

"Dirk. You've been here for two minutes. Don't you tell me how to feel."

Dirk just looked at him. It was obvious he had something to say but thought better of it.

Then Derek turned to William. "And I don't know what you did this evening. But, once I find out, don't think you won't pay."

William started to respond, but Derek pointed to both and continued in his eerily strange voice.

"You will both find out who's truly needed and who is not. William, you are expendable. Everyone knows it. Dirk, it doesn't matter how big your Stetson is. It doesn't make you a man."

Derek stared both astonished men down with an icy glare, backed away from them while still pointing, and slammed the door on his way out. Dirk began shaking his head.

William was the first to break the silence. "That lad just set himself up for a world of heartbreak."

Dirk seemed to shake it out of his system as he responded, "You said it. I'm gonna go for a beer. You?"

The eerie nature of the previous conversation seemed to suck the life out of the room. William, feeling at ease again, turned to Dirk. "No. I'm going to go to the hospital. Thanks for your help. But, watch your back. Derek has decided he doesn't like you. He has proven he can be quite a hothead."

Dirk just chuckled. "Oh, William. Story of my life, man. Story of my life."

Both men walked to their trucks together and went their separate ways.

CHAPTER 6

Dirk Catan sauntered into the Wild Stallion with ease, carrying his Stetson. Like Eli Miller, he just seemed to walk around looking all gorgeous and inflicting his beauty on every able-bodied female in every room. Not once did he ever take notice of the effect he had on anyone.

Dirk was more ruggedly handsome than Eli. He was older, so he did not have the baby face that Eli did. His long, wavy hair was a chestnut color and he had super-broad shoulders that slimmed way down to a very narrow waistline. You could tell those shoulders hadn't become that broad from a gym. Dirk's shoulders were a piece of art from hard work.

His face held a ton of pain, but his glowing heart just peered through. How any woman could cause Dirk any pain was unfathomable. He was the type of man for which every woman fought and saw in her dreams.

Dirk nodded when he saw the familiar face for which he searched. He pulled over a stool, straddled it, and sat down. The woman bartender thought she heard a faint sigh from every single woman in the bar.

"What'll it be, cowboy?" It was her typical remark, but she felt her cheeks blush when Dirk flashed a smile at her.

"Uh? How about a Bud Light? Tap."

"Coming right up!" She couldn't help but flash him a smile back. What was she doing? She was one of the toughest bartenders around! Frustrated with herself, she poured Dirk his beer, took the money he left for her, and left the change.

Dirk looked at Galen Maleno after he took a long drink from his beer. "Haven't been home yet today, have ya?"

Galen didn't look up from his own beer. "If you're asking if I know about the asthma attack, William already texted. He told me he'd keep me informed."

Dirk looked at Galen while he took another swig of beer. He also looked over at the already empty glass in front of him.

"Drowning your sorrows?" Dirk asked.

Galen still didn't look up from his current beer, which was almost finished. "A lot on my mind."

Dirk felt like he was having a conversation with himself at this point. He understood that Galen was having a bad day, but this was very rude, and Dirk was very annoyed. He pinched the brow of his nose and let out a deep breath.

"Gale, you gave me a job and a place to stay when I was hard up. Least I can do is listen, but you have to help me out here a little bit."

His voice trailed off. He hoped that Galen picked up on his hint.

Finally, Galen looked straight ahead, back at his beer, and started swirling the remainder of the beverage in his cup. He finally put it down, turned on the stool, and looked down. Settled, he looked up and sighed. He had a look of desperation in his eyes that Dirk knew all too well.

"I … I miss her. I'm a mess without her."

Dirk looked down himself, searching for the right words. Although this was a sensitive issue for him, he was going to tread through these waters to help his friend, no matter how painful.

"Galen, you *could* just … talk to her."

"Are you going to talk to Mary Ann?" There it was. The most treacherous and awful thing one man could ever say to Dirk.

Galen's sudden defensiveness caused Dirk to become unsure of the nature of the conversation.

Dirk had lived on his wife's family ranch. He came from a poor family but was no stranger to hard work. His wife's family was rich and did not care how hard Dirk worked. He had never been good enough for Mary Ann.

"Come on, brother. Mary Ann is pregnant. You know more than anyone the baby isn't mine. Do you *really* think I should talk to her? Do you really think there's a chance for us? Gale. You know me better than that."

Galen looked at Dirk. He suddenly realized how much his lashing out had hurt Dirk and he felt ashamed. He knew how hard Dirk was trying to put his life back together and he knew what a solid man Dirk was. Galen decided to turn the conversation back to himself.

"She and Catherine just don't understand. They weren't brought up like us. They never took the time to see what kind of men we are."

Galen was suddenly so glad for the one thing that he had received from his broken relationship with Catherine: Dirk.

Mary Ann and Catherine were sisters. They were brainwashed beauties, kept under their father's thumb their entire lives. They both rebelled at times, meeting Galen and Dirk on one of many excursions. But in the end, they were both Daddy's little girls and blood was always thicker than water.

Dirk felt the same way Galen did. "Gale, Catherine never cheated on you, she just pushed you away. She kept you at a distance for your own good. If you think you can deal with that, go get her! You aren't betraying me by doing so."

Galen just looked at Dirk and wondered how a simple ranch hand could be so wise.

Dirk continued. "I put my all into Mary Ann. There was no other way I could have loved her more. There just isn't any more of me I could have put into us. All I did was push her into the arms of another man. I just ... I can't go back. That kind of hurt is just something a man can't withstand."

Dirk took a drink of his beer and swallowed hard before he continued. Gale waited for him to finish talking. What Dirk was saying was exactly what he needed to hear.

"It's who I am, Galen. I know I don't look the part, but it's who I am. I fall hard, and I need someone who falls just as hard."

Gale gave Dirk an understanding smile. "That's why every girl in this bar wants to be on your arm, Dirk."

Dirk laughed a big, hearty laugh. "Gale. I think you've had too much to drink."

Just as the conversation took a more lighthearted turn, Galen reached into his pocket for his ringing cell phone. He took the call as Dirk looked concerned.

"All okay?"

Galen responded. "All okay. My sister is being released from the hospital. Seems to be okay."

Galen paid his tab and arose, grabbing his coat.

Dirk gave him a playful jab and said, "Thanks for the job ... boss!"

Galen playfully jabbed him back and the desperation of the women in the bar could be felt through the air. Two hot guys … one cowboy and one suit. Friends, poking fun on their way out of the bar. What did a girl have to do to even get close to that? It was like the main characters from a Harlequin romance novel had just walked out the door.

Once they reached the porch, Galen's tone turned halfway serious again.

"Dirk, in all seriousness. I'm so glad you're here. It means so much to have a friend close by. I grew up with a lot of strong women. A laid-back friend to have a beer with is worth its weight in gold."

Dirk gave his friend a pat on the back and replied, "Anytime."

As they parted ways and Dirk walked to his truck, something occurred to him. A *lot* of strong women? So far, he only counted two. But, man. The two he counted certainly seemed like a handful.

CHAPTER 7

Driving up the long, winding driveway, Dirk could see a light in the distance toward the stable. So far, he hadn't been able to count one normal day or night at this new place of employment. As he drove closer, he noticed the light was a small bonfire and a small figure was sitting at the bonfire on a log. Driving closer, he recognized the smaller figure. The slender, beautiful frame with dark red hair reminded him of the sparks jumping up out of that very pit. It churned a fire deep within him that he had not felt for quite a while.

"Ms. Lena?"

Lena sighed, exasperated. "It's just Lena, Dirk. Let's keep the formal out of it."

Dirk got the impression that she was called "Miss" a lot and was not especially fond of it. He also picked up on the fact that his new boss was not in a very joyful place of mind.

Dirk looked around a bit before he sat down. Squinting, he looked at the main house and saw a shiny car in the drive. It looked terribly expensive, but he was way too far, and it was way too dark to notice what it was.

Lena frustratingly provided the answer for him. "It's a Rolls Royce. Now stop your squinting." She picked up a stick and started to poke at the fire.

Dirk couldn't believe his eyes. A Rolls Royce! He was sure this ranch was filled with adventures and secrets just waiting to unfold. He walked to the other side of the fire and put a few logs amid the flames.

"You don't seem very happy about your company."

Dirk turned his head to the right as something gray caught his eye. About twenty-five yards from the fire was a tent with an open screen. Inside he could see an air mattress, pillow, and a lantern. He could only guess what kind of shenanigans went on here while he was away.

Dirk had not been gone all that long. He made a mental note for himself. Apparently, things didn't require a very long length of time to kick up in this family.

Dirk sat down for a minute. He wasn't sure if he should let the situation drop or poke at it a little more. Before he could decide, he heard footsteps.

Galen had changed out of his suit and into jeans and a turtleneck. Galen didn't often look like he belonged in this family. The Malenos seemed to be traditional country folks. Galen seemed to be attached to the city in his pressed shirts, Italian leather shoes, and silk ties. Amused, Dirk tried to imagine a childhood between two siblings that were obviously the complete opposite of the other. He looked at Galen's attire again and thought it humorous that at least he had sneakers on.

"Lena. Can we *please* not do this? I'm so tired of this. Whether you like it or not, they are your half sisters. You can pick your friends, but you ..."

Lena jumped right on that sentence before Galen finished it.

"If you complete that sentence, you will regret it, Galen." Lena never looked at him. She snapped at him but never made eye contact. Although they were opposite in personality, it was obvious that Lena and Galen were remarkably close, which intrigued Dirk all the more.

Galen started to pace. It was plausible that he was trying to fix the situation. It was also likely that this was not his first time. Dirk realized Galen was very weary of a life with a fiery sister. As much as Galen comfortably dealt with conflict every day, his rivalry with Lena made him uneasy. He thrived on strife in the courtroom but could not stand it when it came to his sister.

"Lena, she didn't mean it. You know how they are. They never fit in here. I don't know why Daddy put that in the will."

As Galen suddenly noticed the bewildered look on Dirk's face and narrowed his eyes, an idea came to fruition. It was a tactic he had used on his clients many times. Hearing a story from another point of view often forced them to think about things a little differently. He was going to replay the events from the farmhouse for Dirk, forcing Lena to hear the story from his point of view and hoping she would have a fresh outlook.

"Maybe she will listen to a stranger, Dirk. Here is the situation. My three half sisters are inside. Two are twins and one is … well, not the problem, really. The twins and Lena have always been at odds. My mother was in an abusive marriage briefly before she met Daddy. He adopted the girls. They *are* Malenos. They are considered Daddy's just as much as we are."

Lena sat stone-faced, looking into the fire. She took a drink of beer, as if Galen had said nothing. In fact, she was trying to imagine that Galen was in Pittsburgh and not even present.

Exasperated, Galen proceeded.

"In order to receive their inheritance, they have to stay here and work the ranch for three months. At the end of that time, the five of us and Mother will decide what to do with the ranch. This is much different than what Daddy told us."

Galen gave Dirk a moment to process. He decided to focus on Lena again.

"Lena, I saw the document. It's legal and binding. Daddy wants them to make an educated decision."

Lena looked up from the fire slowly and gave Galen a look that clearly stated that she was having no discussion about this tonight. Galen threw up his hands in frustration and walked away, mumbling something about wishing he were an only child.

Dirk remembered Galen's former remark about growing up around a lot of strong women. It was all becoming crystal clear.

As Galen walked away, Dirk decided to move closer to Lena. The workings of this family completely captivated him.

"May I?"

Dirk took a beer from the cooler as Lena shrugged indifferently. Both sat in silence and stared into the fire for quite a while.

Lena snuck a sideways glance to examine Dirk's strong jawline and shoulders. Sitting beside her was another man who had no idea how incredibly beautiful he really was. Why did she always attract those sorts of men?

Irritated, she remarked, "Why are you here?"

Dirk answered her simply. "I needed a job. You gave me one."

Lena rolled her eyes. She was really in no mood for anyone that was in a better mood.

"No. I mean why are you *here*. As in by my fire."

Dirk was suddenly embarrassed by his mistake. "Would you like me to go?"

Lena suddenly squirmed in her seat. She wished she were a meaner person like the twins.

She thought for a minute of a more diplomatic thing to say. "I'm afraid I'm not very good company this evening."

Dirk decided to challenge her comment. Recently, being the least popular member of a family had taught him to be very witty with answers. "Do people always have to be the best of company to be friends?"

Lena looked up into beautiful green eyes that glistened in the fire.

Suspiciously, she remarked, "You want to be my friend."

Dirk was not going to allow her to disengage that easily.

"Well. I live here now. I like it here. Don't you think it would be easier if we were friends? Within reason, of course … considering …"

Lena looked thoughtfully at Dirk. Trust was out of the box for her. She decided to allow just a little trust out of the bag while breaking down any walls.

"I guess I could give a little."

Dirk suddenly perked up. Lena thought he was just a little too peppy for her at a moment's notice.

"Great! Be right back."

Peppy or not, watching Dirk Catan walk away was like watching a racehorse run. He walked with long, sexy strides at a fast pace, gliding along with strength and purpose. It was hot as hell.

When he returned, he was carrying a bedroll and a gun, as if he'd walked right off the set of *Bonanza*.

Lena just stared at him for a moment before she spoke. "What do you think you're doing?"

Dirk smiled. "Coyotes. I'm sleeping under the stars tonight. Besides. It is a gorgeous night. Don't you think so?"

That was it. There was no possible way this man was in constant cheer! Lena just couldn't bear it.

Cynically, Lena looked at him with incredulous eyes. "Do you think I can't take care of myself? What kind of game are you playing?"

Dirk looked at her, pleased with himself. It only enraged Lena more. Dirk suddenly realized he should watch his step. It was hard for Lena to trust, which perplexed him. After all that had happened to him, Dirk was still able to see the good in the world.

"Lena, I have no doubt you can take care of yourself. But, if we are going to do this friend thing, I am going to show you I am a great guy to have as a friend. So, good night."

Looking at him very suspiciously, Lena walked back to her tent. "Really. Okay then. We'll see. Good night, Dirk." She crawled into her tent and slowly zipped it up.

Dirk grinned to himself. He liked a challenge.

CHAPTER 8

Waking up well-rested, Lena could smell something delightful wafting through her tent. She also heard some unexpected giggling and talking. Expecting the worst, she decided to pull on her boots and go outside.

Dirk and a familiar face were locked in conversation, much to her surprise. When Lena's sister, Allie, had left Daddy's funeral, she was wearing glasses that were way bigger than her face, had a short, spiky pixie cut that made her look like a boy, a frumpy dress that was two sizes too big, no makeup, and shoes that looked like orthopedic shoes. That was not the girl having breakfast with Dirk. This girl was a natural beauty with long, red hair a few shades lighter than Lena's. There were no glasses. The clothes she wore hugged her small frame, showing off her petite figure. The makeup she wore was simple but brought out her best features.

"Allie? Is that you? What are you doing out here?"

Allie whirled around, obviously not expecting to see her younger sister standing there.

Allison Maleno was the middle child, always quiet and mousy. She had grown up with her nose in a book, the slave of her older twin sisters, which often annoyed Lena. Allie never stood up for herself and would often retreat to different places on the ranch to read and hide from the twins. She always wore her hair short, which was easiest to manage. She never cared about herself enough to buy nice clothes, much to their mother's dismay. The closest person to her was Lena, but they had still had a guarded relationship through childhood. Allie never let anyone into her world and Lena was too young to figure out how to break through.

Now, Lena was looking into the face of a beauty. Allie's hair was chestnut red and shone in the sun like silk. She had bangs and an even smaller frame than Lena, but they looked a lot alike. Allie looked more fragile and petite. Lena knew Allison certainly had a bigger heart than she did and was more sensitive.

"Hi, Lena! I felt so badly about the horrible things Gracie said to you. I brought some warm bagels, bacon, and coffee out here and found Dirk! We were just laughing and joking around."

No matter how hard she tried, Lena could not help but genuinely love Allie, who was the sweetest and most elegant of the Maleno women. Allie had no idea that Gracie's words had hit harder than ever. *You think you're better because you're Daddy's true daughter.* Even though that was no longer true, Lena was not about to give Gracie the satisfaction of the truth.

"Ah, Allie. That's so sweet. Thank you. I've missed you!" She embraced Allie.

Dirk was smiling at the whole scene. Lena could tell in this small amount of time, he was already curious about Allie and quite taken with her.

"Lena, you wanted to show me the other trails today. Shall I saddle up two of the trail horses?"

Lena stretched. She hadn't quite finished her coffee, so she didn't feel fully awake quite yet. "Oh. Yes, Dirk. Please allow me to freshen up for just a bit. Then I'll join you. See if Hunter has come in yet, then we will be off."

Allie could barely contain herself as Lena finished her sentence. She danced around like a five-year-old. Lena looked at her with a wicked grin on her face.

"Uh. Lena?"

Lena was entertained by the excitement she had never seen in Allie before. In fact, the whole idea of this sudden friendship between Dirk and Allie made her smile. She felt it was her duty to play the role of overprotective sister.

"Yes?"

Allie danced around a little more, obviously extremely nervous about something. Looking away from Allie, Lena tried not to laugh out loud.

"Well, come on, Allie! Spit it out!" There was sudden shock on Lena's face as she realized how much she just sounded like her mother.

Allie just smiled, then started rambling and talking extremely fast.

"Well … maybe I could join you? I mean … it said in the will that we're to stay here all summer … so, maybe I would like to show interest in the trail riding. And, I should get to know the trails too, you know? In case you need me to do that! And, I should really learn how to ride properly and …"

Lena just looked at Allie, dumbfounded. Allie was a better rider than Lena! During their childhood, it was Allie who had spent most of her life on a horse. She rode off for hours with nothing but a sandwich, a bottle of water, and a book. It was Allie that would show Lena the trails. Lena couldn't believe what she was hearing. The person who knew this land better than anyone was Allison Maleno.

Dirk suddenly interrupted Lena's train of thought.

"Lena, would that be okay?"

Lena just looked at him, shaking herself out of her daydream.

"Huh? I'm sorry, Dirk. Come again?"

Dirk repeated himself. "I said, I could show Allie all about saddling up a horse and such."

Not able to stop herself, Lena just laughed out loud. "Um, Dirk ..."

Allie looked pleadingly at Lena. Lena was loving how the tables had turned. Allie had certainly come out of her shell. Lena thought it was so endearing that she did not have the heart to come up with the truth.

Laughing, Lena answered. "Dirk, go right ahead."

Dirk looked at her suspiciously. He looked like he knew he was missing something, but he decided not to pursue it.

Dirk needed this, too. He needed to be needed. His green eyes shone emerald again and Allie looked at him with pure admiration, causing Lena to snicker to herself as she pictured a champion rider getting a novice riding lesson. Lena just shook her head.

Lena's snicker was short-lived. Something caught her eye from over the hill, so she shaded her eyes. Suddenly, her heart began to beat faster, and her palms began to sweat. Lena gave herself a pep talk, telling herself to play it cool as Eli continued to saunter down the field.

"Eli! No truck today? How are you?"

Eli walked up to Lena and smiled. "No truck today. I'm fine. Thank you, Lena."

Lena felt that wasn't the whole truth, but she didn't want to pry. She just followed Eli into the barn.

"I was just going to clean up a bit, but I wanted to warn you, Eli—"

Before she could finish, there it was.

"Why, Eli Miller, as I live and breathe! As if you could be any more dashing!"

Eli stopped in his tracks. The sound cut like a knife. Eli closed his eyes for a moment, then turned around with utter horror on his face.

Charlotte. Twin number one and the more toxic of the two. She was also the most stunningly gorgeous of all the Maleno children.

Charlie, as she preferred to be called, was the person responsible for crushing Eli's heart a while ago. Charlotte Maleno was a doppelganger to Marilyn Monroe. Everywhere she went, people turned their heads twice and stared. Charlie ate it up.

Eli swallowed hard and pretended that she was a client.

"Miss Charlotte. Glad to see you are well."

That answer did not satisfy the brazen Charlie. Lena felt weak in the knees, as if she were watching a tornado coming straight for her and she was frozen in place. She could not run for cover.

Eli began to reach for his hat, but Charlie was too fast. She grabbed the hat out of his hands, slowly turning Eli toward her. Lena felt her stomach turn as Charlie rubbed Eli's V-neck shirt, then his shoulders, then down his arms until she caught his hands. She pulled his hands to her chest and pulled him close. Eli was white as a ghost. Charlie still had power over Eli, and it made Lena's heart sink.

"I can't believe it's possible for a man to get even more handsome, Eli! I believe you need to take me out to dinner so we can catch up."

Lena watched as Charlie's mouth moved so close to Eli's that it was impossible for him to ignore her breath on his neck.

He could smell her intoxicating perfume that was putting him in a trance. He had vowed never to be here again.

"Charlie!"

Lena did not even feel the bile bubbling up from her stomach at first, nor did she feel the rage coming out of her mouth. Surprisingly, she could not believe it was her voice that produced the word so toxically.

Lena's curt remark was so deafening that Charlie almost fell when she turned on her heel. "Why, little sister! Are you enjoying the show over there? I was getting reacquainted with my man!"

Lena was almost boiling over at this point. The furor had engulfed her and now she was aiming right for Charlie.

"Oh really? I'll reacquaint you. Your man was gone all weekend for his mother's funeral. I am sorry. Were you not privy to the arrangements? Forget your black dress to comfort 'your man' while he grieved? Maybe it's in the closet with the broom you rode in on."

Eli decided this would be a great time to pick up his tools and leave the barn. Trying to back out of the line of fire as quietly as possible, he loaded his tools into his box and started for the door. An obvious sister-to-sister face-off was imminent and he was not sure he had the strength for it.

Charlie, obviously ignoring the insult hurled at her, was focused on the funeral. "You're lying."

Lena took her opportunity to show Charlie how serious she truly was, and that she was no longer a little girl that could be pushed around anymore. She was not going to play the role of littlest sister any longer.

Lena walked up to Charlie, who was a good five inches taller, and planted her stance. Lena did not back down.

"I'm not. You're selfish, and you need to stay away from Eli Miller."

The two sisters stared at each other for a few seconds before another strong voice entered the barn. Charlie grinned slowly, obviously ready to unleash a wild frenzy of her own on her youngest sister. Lena knew she was outrivaled, but this time she was going to go down fighting.

"I think that would be wise, Charlie."

Recognizing the voice, both sisters looked over to see Lois standing there with her arms crossed. The look on her face was scolding and disapproving. Lena recognized it right away. Lois rarely had to raise her voice or even give a lecture. She had "the look." When Lois gave you her look of disapproval, it was worse than any form of punishment. Lena had to admit that she was slightly pleased that Charlie was the recipient of it now. Dirk and Allison, outside the barn, had witnessed everything and had gone to get Lois or Galen, whoever they could find.

Charlie suddenly changed her tune. Backing away from Lena, she suddenly smiled, obviously thinking she could sweet-talk her mother out of this.

"Mother! I was just …"

Lois was not deterred. When Lois was in this mindset, nothing could distract her. Lois was tough. When you did wrong, you knew it. The Maleno children had grown up learning respect. This was a moment to tread lightly, and Charlie knew it.

"I know what you were trying to do, Charlotte Faith. Eli Miller and every other man on this ranch are off-limits to you. I mean it." Lois' voice was flat and cold as she walked up to Charlie and looked her in the eye. The phrase was slow and deliberate. Charlie knew that even one more word would be the wrong one.

Charlie, obviously embarrassed, stomped out of the barn like a child and slammed the door.

Lena broke into a smile.

"Mama, thank you. I was just ..." Lena immediately realized her miscalculation. The look was not just for Charlie and it did not vanish just because Charlie did. This time, the punishing disappointment was directed at her, and Lena despised it. Lois did not intend to give Lena a break, either. In two seconds, the look was turned on her.

"As for you. We do not run off with tents and stay away from our problems. Your father would hate that."

Lena still had a little leftover fury inside of her. She felt fierce and reckless. In her childhood, one never dreamed of backtalking Lois Maleno. It just was not done. But Lena was no longer a child. Her next remark was cool and meant to cut like a knife.

"Which father would that be, Mother?"

This time it was Lena that stomped out of the barn, slamming the door.

Lois stood in the middle of the barn. She lowered her head into her hands and cried, knowing that the level of respect Lena once had for her was gone.

CHAPTER 9

Lena walked down the path to the barn, watching as Allie and Dirk were obviously getting quite comfortable with one another. Everything about their body language claimed they were crazy about each other. Lena might have chuckled about the odd pairing if she was not so distraught.

"Dirk, I'm so very sorry. I'm afraid I can't do this today. I have a family issue that needs my immediate attention." She hoped he could hear the disappointment in her voice. She would much rather be on a horse than dealing with everything else in her life at this moment. She wanted Dirk to know that.

Dirk and Allie both looked extremely disappointed by the news and she could tell that riding was something they had both anticipated. Lena could understand why Allie enjoyed Dirk's company. Not only was he drop-dead gorgeous, but he was kind and sweet. Lena wondered how two of the kindest souls she knew could possibly make it in this world. She always felt that Allison needed to be protected.

Lena was startled by a soft touch on her shoulder and turned to see that warm smile she always remembered of Allie's before she turned into this nearly unrecognizable supermodel.

"Lena? I remember the trail to the old fire tower. I used to go there to read when things got heated around here. I remember it well. If you trust me, could I show Dirk the trail?"

Lena wondered if Dirk had caught on to Allie by now. She smiled to herself when she thought about how Allie's "first saddle lesson" had gone. Certainly, Allie would have come clean when she was not successful at pulling off the whole "I don't know anything" act. Lena imagined Dirk to be too smart for such nonsense.

It had been several years since Allie had ridden the trail to the fire tower and it was not very worn anymore. Lena had wanted to break the trail in again. She didn't know if sending Allie on a partially grown-in trail was wise.

Lena's sisters had all gone away to a residential private school, then college. It was Lena who refused to leave the ranch, or her father, which defined her as the wild one. She had been sent away one time, had gotten into trouble by running away, and the school had sent her home. Ren Maleno had never sent her back. Lena was always Daddy's little girl and her sisters knew that, so they never fought when Lena stayed home and attended public school.

"I don't know about this, Allie. The trails are partially grown in. They aren't as worn as you remember. It will be easy for you to get lost."

Allie looked at Lena. It was the first time Lena noticed a strength about her. "Lena. Do you realize how many times I have ridden that trail?" Ah. So she *had* come clean to Dirk about knowing how to ride. "That fire tower was *my* favorite place and that trail was worn by me more than anyone else. I promise you. There is no possible way that I would forget it."

Lena smiled, realizing that Allie was right. It was her hideout when they were children. Allie had built an entire camp at the end of that road as her territory. If Allie was missing, Lena knew where to find her.

Lena smiled. "Okay, Allie. I suppose you are right. I will leave my cell on. Leave Myrna saddled in case you get lost and I will come right away for you."

Allie hugged Lena. "Thank you, Lena." Allie knew that this was a trust test for Lena. This ranch meant everything to her. Allie had returned, but that didn't mean that Lena trusted her anymore. She didn't have the heart in it that Lena had.

Turning to Dirk, Allie asked, "Dirk, will this be okay with you? Oh I'm sorry. I should have asked that first!"

Dirk looked so longingly at her, it caused Lena to cover her mouth. She wanted so badly to tease her sensitive sister. But she knew Allie would take it to heart.

Dirk looked down and put his forehead on Allie's, smiling. "Absolutely. I would go anywhere with you." Lena thought she was just about to witness their first kiss. She stood very quietly, hoping they were so lost in the moment, they forgot her presence.

Dirk picked up his head and looked over at Lena, beginning to stutter, embarrassed by his vulnerability. "Besides. I left plenty for Hunter to do. And well, Derek doesn't speak to me … so …"

Lena looked back at him with concern. "I'll talk to him."

She honestly didn't know what to do about Derek. He was good help, but he was a ticking time bomb with his furious temper. He was young and wanted to take on the world. She couldn't begrudge him that. Yet, he scared her to some extent. If Derek couldn't control his temper, she would have no choice but to send him home. His crush was beginning to make her uncomfortable, and his temper was just adding fuel to the fire.

Dirk could tell by Lena's small, choked response that she didn't really want to do that. It was obvious to him that Derek's actions were making Lena question the boy's employment on the ranch. "Lena, no need to talk to young Derek. It will all work itself out, the cowboy way. You just leave it alone and let us men figure it out."

Lena smiled at the thought, and Dirk was pleased his comment seemed to perk her up. "If you say so! Thank you, Dirk."

Lena smiled coyly to Allie, who returned the look with surprise. "What was that for?"

Lena just winked. "No reason. You two be careful. In every sense of the word!" Lena winked again at Allie, who returned her comment with her hands on her hips.

"Well, I never!"

Dirk let out a deep, hearty laugh. He enjoyed being around the two redheaded sisters.

Lena decided to proceed to the stables, knowing it was time for Eli to be working with Maddox, one of the newer colts on the ranch.

Walking into the stables cautiously, Lena could tell that Eli was spooked by Charlie. She would have to play this smart to not unnerve him any further.

Eli was smiling as the colt ran about, obviously happy to watch him play in the meadow. Lena decided to walk up and sit on the fence behind him as she often did. "Howdy!"

Eli turned around, surprised. "Lena!"

Eli looked to make sure the colt was not in danger, then walked over to the fence.

Lena began to say something, until Eli's hand silenced her. "Stop. Let me guess. You're sorry about Charlie. You came to warn me. You didn't expect her to be here and you're sorry if you said anything to offend me. Am I close?"

Lena could feel her cheeks glowing a bright red. She instantly put her hands on her warm cheeks. "Yeah. You are dead on."

Eli pulled her hands down from her cheeks and held both of her hands in his own. "Lena ..." His voice trailed off as he searched for the words. "Look. I was different before. More naïve when Charlotte and I ..." He looked away, closed his eyes, then looked back at Lena before he proceeded. "I'm not likely to trot down that path again. She still pushes my buttons. But I know what she's all about."

Eli was both a little surprised and disappointed in himself. He wasn't the type to put himself out there like this. He was so disappointed that he had allowed Charlotte Maleno to turn him into a huge pile of goo again, and this time it was right in front of Lena. He hated that she still had that power over him.

"And me? Is our friendship to pay the price for the sins of my sister?" Lena looked at him with tears forming in her eyes.

Eli sighed. His words were not coming out as he intended, and everything was becoming distorted. He walked over to the fence and put his arms on the rail and his chin on his arms, deep in thought for a few moments. Turning his head, he looked at Lena, who was wiping tears away from her eyes.

"Will you take a drive with me, Lena?"

Stunned, Lena dried her last tear and looked at him. "Where?"

Eli held out a hand to help her down. "Would it be creepy for you not to know where? I'd like you to just trust me. There's something I'd like to show you. I'm hoping it will help you understand ..." Eli's voice trailed off.

Lena put her hand in his and started for the truck.

"Hold on!" Eli chuckled. "There's a horse in the middle of a field! A young one!"

At that moment, William headed toward them. Noticing Lena and Eli hand in hand, William started to grin. "Goin' somewhere?"

Lena instantly looked down. The relationship between Lena and William was strained right now. She was confused and didn't know what to do.

Eli could feel the tension between the two, but he had a mission. "Well, that was our intention. But I have to—"

William jumped on his sentence before he finished. "No worries, Eli. I've got him."

"Are you sure?"

William tried to get Lena to look at him, but Lena was suddenly enthralled with the colt that was so intently frolicking in the pasture. Not wanting to deal with the William issue right now, she just smiled at him awkwardly.

"Absolutely. You two have a nice afternoon. I've got this."

Lena knew William was hoping to gain points with this gesture.

Eli had no idea of William's intentions; he was just grateful that William was doing him a favor. Eli thanked William and led Lena to the old beat-up pickup truck.

The door screeched as Eli opened it and helped Lena inside. Lena thought it was chivalrous when he took her by the waist and so easily hoisted her up into the passenger seat. She liked that feeling and wondered if Eli meant to do that or even noticed. Eli was so polite, and he probably had no idea of the effect these little things had on her, Lena surmised.

After about ten minutes of driving, Eli turned down a long, winding road and pulled over. There was an old lumber mill that hadn't been used in years. Eli pulled into the lot and just sat there.

Confused, Lena looked around. This seemed like a very odd place to just hang out. Although an exquisite setting, it was not exactly the most private place. Lena wasn't quite sure why Eli would bring her to an old, dilapidated mill. "Eli, I don't quite understand what's going on."

Eli pointed to a farmhouse on a rolling hillside. "Those are my brothers and sisters."

Lena could see Amish kids coming out of the house on the hill. Older girls were bringing out laundry and hanging it on the clothesline. Two little boys were riding bikes up and down the hill. A dog was chasing them.

Eli's face grew proud. "The oldest girl is Rachel. She can make the best banana bread in the entire world, I swear. The girl next to her, hanging clothes on the line, is Esther. She's the shy one." Lena watched and listened as Eli proudly told her about each one of his siblings. "Now, that young lad that just rolled down the hill and who is now getting scolded by Rachel is Zeke. He's the rebellious one." Eli turned to look at Lena, eyes bright and shining. "I bet you thought I was the rebellious one." Lena chuckled, but she did not dare say anything, wanting this mood in Eli to continue. "Now, the furry one is Spud."

Lena scrunched up her nose. "Spud?"

Eli laughed. "Zeke named him. When he was a puppy, he kept getting into Mama's potato bin. Mama would yell, 'Get out of my spuds!' Zeke thought it was hysterical. Thus, Spud."

Lena giggled. "That is a great name for a dog."

Lena just continued to look at the darling siblings as Eli continued. This was the most Lena had ever heard him say at one time. "The little tyke that just pretended to wrestle with Spud is Micah. Micah always tries to outrun Spud, but he just can't yet." As if on cue, Micah, a little blond boy of about three, tried to run across the lawn and was instantly tackled by a golden retriever as Eli watched in amazement. Lena watched him. The look on his face warmed her heart.

The little boys came over to the truck and Eli opened the door. The girls pretended not to notice as they continued with the laundry. Lena decided they knew where the boys were. A bounding Spud came to the door as well. Eli came out of the truck to greet them.

"Ewhy! Ewhy!" Micah had his hands up, wanting Eli to pick him up. Unfortunately, so did Spud.

"Spud, get down. Hey there, li'l man! How are you?"

Micah beamed. "Ewhy, Rachel make-ted my pancakes."

Eli put his forehead on Micah's. "I bet they were very delicious."

Micah whispered, "Not as delicious as the angel pancakes."

Eli looked up at him, confused. "The angel pancakes?"

Zeke filled in the blanks. "Esther told him that *Mamm* now makes pancakes for the angels."

Eli choked up for a moment, then continued. "Ohhhhh … but I bet Rachel's pancakes were still tasty."

Zeke curiously went to Lena's side of the truck. "Who are you?"

Lena put her window down. "Hello! You're Zeke, right?" Zeke's face lit up as he looked at Eli. "Your brother told me all about you!"

Zeke got a sour look on his face. "Are you the reason Hannah, Rachel, and Rebecca don't talk to Eli?"

Eli instantly got down to the boys' level. "Boys, we talked about this. This is Lena. She is my friend, but I did not know Lena when everyone stopped talking to me. It is nice of them to let you talk to me, and you must not be mad at anyone that refuses me. We will talk of all these things another time. It's time to go back."

Zeke and Micah both had a sad look on their face, but they understood. They hugged their big brother and ran to the house. Suddenly, Esther called, "Eli, stop."

Eli stopped in disbelief. Esther had not called to him in many years. Rachel had taken the boys into the house.

"Esther?"

She had an envelope in her hand.

"This will be the only time we speak. I have been waiting for a time when *Daed* is not here and you stop to see your brothers. This was in *Mamm's* Bible. That is your name. We all have one." Esther presented Eli with a letter. Eli's eyes filled with tears. "She had the sickness for months. She did not tell us …" Esther did not finish her sentence but turned and walked back to the house.

Lena realized Eli had probably been shunned by his family. The death of his mother had been harder on him than anyone because he had not been allowed to see her. Eli had been banished because he had left his religion, his community, and his family.

As Eli read the letter, tears streamed down his cheeks, and Lena's heart broke for him. After he finished, he looked at her. "Would you like to know what it says?"

Lena held out her hand. "I can just read it for myself, if it's too hard for you."

Eli shook his head. "It's in German."

Lena tilted her head. "Whatever you want, Eli."

Eli thought for a moment. "It is a way for you to know my family. You will never meet my mother."

Lena held his hand. "Okay, Eli. What does the letter say?"

Eli began reading.

My Elijah,
I am a sick woman and will be leaving you soon. I regret that
I did not hold you one last time. I know it is not our way, but you
are my Eli. I love you still. I know you look on your siblings in secret.
Please continue to make sure they are safe. I did not stop loving you.
I never will.
Maam.

He folded the letter, dried his eyes, and put the letter above
the visor in his truck. He turned and looked at Lena.

Lena's heart ached as she looked at the house, then back
at Eli. Micah was in the window, waving furiously. Eli smiled
back and returned the little boy's wave with a smile on his face.
She wondered how many times he came here and watched
them. Suddenly, Micah switched with Zeke, who gave a small,
sheepish wave. Eli waved back. The little boys continued playing
with Spud in the window.

"Oh, Eli. I had no idea!"

Eli looked away from his family and back at Lena. "I would
like you to keep it that way. Please pretend, Lena."

Lena looked into those eyes, stricken with pain. "Of
course. But why did you tell me?"

Eli's face turned pale. It was obvious he was holding back
tears and sorrow. "Because when my mother died, I felt so alone,
and you were there. You are right. You are nothing like your sister.
I wanted to do something to show you that I didn't think that."

Lena was so touched by that sentiment. His display of trust
was the most heartwarming thing anyone had ever done for her.
She could feel her cheeks flush and her hand rise to her chest.

Eli continued. "Lena, I want to be honest."

Lena didn't know what to say. "Eli, I'm so honored. Thank you for trusting me. This is such a gift."

Lena flew into his arms. His arms wrapped around her in exchange and she could feel her heart take flight. Things between Lena Maleno and Eli Miller were exactly where they were meant to be.

CHAPTER *10*

On the way home, there was a lot of hand-holding and a lot of smiling. Lena felt like she was in high school again. Her stomach had butterflies over and over while Eli pointed out things he loved in nature. Lena thought this was just about as close to heaven as a person could ever get.

When Lena and Eli pulled into the driveway, they encountered a very fired-up Derek. They both bailed out of the truck in record time.

"I do *not* take orders from *you!*"

Lena's heart sank. So much for her perfect afternoon. It didn't take long to figure out where this was going. She looked to the left and found another twin sister—Gracie, toxic twin; the sequel.

"What a mouth you have! I like it. You're all full of fire, little one!" Gracie was not quite Marilyn Monroe, but she was just as gorgeous. She was tall and had a slimmer build than Charlie. Her hair was usually shorter and curlier. There was no denying the fact that although Charlie had the curves and celebrity good looks, Gracie was just as stunning.

She rubbed her hand up and down Derek's chest, prompting him to bolt away from her like her hands were on fire. Gracie's eyes danced as she accepted this new challenge.

Derek was obviously uncomfortable. Gracie liked puzzles. It was the thrill of the chase for her, and Derek Hopstef was a formidable opponent.

Eli stepped in just in time.

"Derek, come with me." Eli tried to put his arm around Derek and lead him away, but Gracie butted in, inserting herself between the two men.

"Oh, Derek, is it? Such a strong name. What is that you do here? Do you break horses or something?"

Derek, as always, wasn't one to leave a fight. "I think I need to stay right here!"

Gracie's eyes lit up with intrigue. "Oh really. I think you should stay here as well."

Derek pumped his hands in frustration. "That's not what I meant."

Gracie put her finger on his lips. "I think that's exactly what you meant."

Derek bolted across the room.

Lena was frustrated. Derek was out of his league in a battle of wits with Gracie. She wanted to tell him that, but Gracie would just end up being proud that Lena thought so highly of her.

Eli cautiously approached Derek as if he were a spooked horse. "Derek. Do you trust me? Have I ever led you astray?"

Derek looked at Eli for a moment before he answered. "No, Eli." Reluctantly, Derek looked away from Gracie. Lena could see Gracie recalculating her next move in her head as if there were a GPS there.

"Then come help me with Angel Dust. I need someone who is familiar with her."

"I could come too, then we could all become familiar with each other!" Gracie was about to move toward them when Lena stepped in front of her.

"Knock it off, Gracie." Lena was curt and to the point.

Gracie did not want to fight, she just wanted to tease. "Lena, I never realized how many gorgeous men are on this ranch! And they all work for me! This is a dream come true!"

Lena did not move. She just shook her head and whispered to Gracie, "Who *are* you?"

Gracie moved around Lena and sat on a hay bale. "Oh relax, Lena. I'm not moving in on your territory. That one that you and Charlie pine over ain't my type."

Lena marched over to Gracie, who pulled some gum out of her pocket and began to unwrap it. Lena yanked the gum out of her hand and tossed it across the barn. "Why do you and Charlie treat people this way? It's like we aren't related at all!"

Gracie just rolled her eyes and rose. "Like you ever pretended to be, Lena. Please. You are the chosen child. The rest of us are just the practice children. You know it, Charlie knows it, and I know it. Don't behave as if you weren't brought up to be better than us. We all play a role in this family, and we all behave as such." With that, Gracie picked up her gum and left.

Gracie's words cut like a knife. Lena had no idea the twins really felt that way. Did Allie feel that way as well? Lena didn't feel like she was the chosen child at all. Why did they feel that way about her?

With Myrna saddled, Lena decided to check some fence posts Hunter had worked on earlier that week. She needed some time away.

CHAPTER *11*

Lena ended up at her favorite spot in the world. It was a flat spot under a willow tree on the riverbank outside the fence. Allie had her spot by the fire tower, but the willow tree was Lena's. She even named it Willow Rose because there was a wild rosebush a few feet away that she could smell from the house in the spring. She loved to camp here. It was her favorite spot on Earth.

Throwing rocks into the lake while she was thinking, she heard a twig crack. Getting up and turning around in the blink of an eye, she saw him. "Eli, how did you …"

Eli smiled back at her. "There's another secret about me. I'm secretly a stalker."

Lena grinned at him questioningly. Eli was not much of a talker, and he certainly did not make too many jokes. Flirtatious Eli Miller?

"Okay, I'm obviously kidding. I saw Hunter. Derek and I helped him bring back supplies. I thought Derek could use the time out fixing fences. William told me what happened and said he didn't need me. He could handle it with just Derek and Hunter."

At that moment, Eli and Lena heard a sound off in the distance …

"Lllleeeeeeeennnnnnnnnaaaaaaaaa!!!!!!!"

It was one of the twin sisters. Lena had not been around them enough to be able to decipher their voices.

"Oh, just peachy. I'm not in the mood to put up with either of them today."

Eli took her hand. "Well, it just so happens that there's another reason I'm coming through here. I am supposed to ride north to help the Farnsworths with a new foal they're expecting. You have anything on your schedule? Molly, the mama mare, had lots of trouble delivering last time."

"Lllllllllleeeeeeeeeeennnnnnnnnnnnaaaaaaaa!!!!!!!!!!!"

"Ugh. I'm supposed to go to lunch with my sisters today and bond."

Eli looked disappointed. "Oh okay. I completely understand. Family first."

Lena hoisted herself onto Myrna, her beautiful blue roan horse. Eli stared at her and Lena recognized the look. She had seen it only once before. It was the same look he'd had when he was on her porch the morning his mother died and she had taken her cap off, revealing her hair as it tumbled down her back. Butterflies always formed in her stomach when Eli looked at her that way. She imagined the goofy look on her face and the color of her cheeks at that moment. Eli looked away and shook his head, as if trying to break his own concentration.

"Okay, to the Farnsworth farm it is. I can*not* deal with my sisters today."

Eli chuckled. "Are you absolutely sure?"

"LLLLLLEEEEEENNNNNNAAAAA! This is the last time I'm calling for you, you little twit!"

Lena just looked at Eli with big eyes. "Uh, yeah. I'm absolutely sure!"

With that, Eli mounted his Appaloosa, Lakota. Lena could see his muscles bulging through his jeans. He had a green plaid shirt on that was open halfway down his chest. As he put his hat on, he tilted it enough to bare those sparkling turquoise eyes that seemed to look deep into her soul. Under that hat were a few wisps of misbehaved blond curls.

"Follow me, I know a shortcut."

Oh, anywhere, Eli Miller, Lena thought to herself. *I would follow you anywhere.*

They rode for about an hour before reaching the Farnsworth ranch. Mrs. Farnsworth, a widow, told Eli that Molly, their mare, had just gone into labor and was already having difficulties.

"I've got it, Ellie. Go into the house and feed the kids. Molly will be fine with Lena and me."

Entering the stall, Lena could see Molly pawing at the ground. It looked like she had already dropped and was ready to give birth.

Eli approached slowly and talked in a cooing manner. He was so soft and gentle with Molly, it made Lena smile. "Hey there, Miss Molly. You ready to meet your little one today?"

"Lena, can you …" Eli looked at the doors and Lena understood.

"On it!" He wanted no interruptions for Molly from the other animals or from the children. Lena went about locking the others outside so Molly could have some privacy. Then, she went in search of water and towels.

During the process, Molly lay down, stood back up, and finally decided on lying down. During this time, her water broke.

Eli was still just as gentle as could be, which impressed Lena.

"Okay. Now, Miss Molly, what seems to be the trouble?" Lena could see the trouble as only one hoof appeared. Eli talked Lena and Molly through the situation as if he were reading a recipe for baking cookies. "Okay, Lena. I'm going to help her out and pull out the other foot. Will you go up by her head and keep her calm? Just talk to her and put her head in your lap, but be careful if she picks it up quickly. Don't let her catch you in the chin."

Lena did as she was told. She stroked Molly's hair and tried to keep the same tone and inflection of voice as Eli, feeling like she was rambling to poor Molly. Molly just kept puffing little breaths and blinking. Lena guessed that was a good sign since Eli didn't say anything.

A few minutes later, Eli cooed softly.

"Why, Mama Molly! Seems you delivered yourself a little girl! You can let her go now, Lena."

Eli placed the foal by her mama and went toward the house to wash up. He announced the news to Mrs. Farnsworth, who mentioned again that she could not do it without him. She gave him an entire bag of baked goods as payment.

Eli just smiled at Mrs. Farnsworth. "Well, Mrs. Farnsworth, if you keep making me all of these lovely things to eat, I won't be able to make it over here to help you anymore!" Lena thought it incredible that Eli was teasing the older woman.

"Oh you hush up. You could use some more meat on those bones, Eli!" Mrs. Farnsworth enjoyed fussing over Eli, which made Lena wonder how much time Eli spent helping families in the community.

"Thank you, Ellie. We best be getting back. Call if you need me again."

Mrs. Farnsworth nodded.

"It was so nice to meet you, Mrs. Farnsworth," Lena said.

"Now, if you are a good friend to Eli, there will be no calling me Mrs. Farnsworth! You call me Ellie, child. And here are some treats for you. You definitely need to fatten up a bit!"

Lena just laughed. "Thank you, ma'am. You are so kind."

"Please come visit."

"I will. Thank you … Ellie!"

Lena's heart was light. She'd made the right decision, coming here instead of going out with her sisters.

Lena could hear her stomach grumble as she and Eli rode back. Eli stopped by Willow Rose and dismounted.

"What are we doing?" Lena asked.

"Well, since you didn't meet with those spirited sisters of yours for lunch, I figured we may as well look in these bags. Ellie is one of the best cooks I know."

Eli motioned for Lena to come closer. He handed her one bag and he took the other. Lena took out a giant corn muffin and a small loaf of pumpernickel bread, which was still warm.

"Good choices!" Eli laughed as he looked in his bag. Eli pulled out a blueberry muffin and a small loaf of rye bread. There was also some sweet butter. Eli pulled out his pocketknife. "Butter?"

Lena turned up her nose, knowing that cowboys used their pocketknife for everything. "I'll pass."

Eli shrugged his shoulders. "Suit yourself."

Time passed in silence as Lena and Eli ate. They were both starving and focused on eating.

Once Lena was satiated, she turned to Eli. "Can I ask you a personal question?"

"Depends. I sometimes answer personal questions. No guarantees."

"Fair enough. How in the world did you get mixed up with my sister, Charlotte?"

Eli almost choked on the drink he was taking from his canteen.

"Okay. I'll answer, but only under one condition."

Ugh. Lena hated conditions to pretty much anything.

"Oh? What's that?" Lena asked, very unenthusiastically.

"You make a better effort to get to know your siblings. Each one. Even Galen. They all have another side to them that they aren't willing to show you. There's a reason for that, if you're willing to listen, Lena."

Lena didn't think she liked where this was going. It was kind of like being ten years old and being forced to eat your Brussel sprouts.

"Go on. I'm listening."

"Your father always treated you differently, Helena. You are different from the others. Your heart is on this ranch. Your siblings won't let their guard down because they see the strength of your two parents in you. You are a force. You can't help it. You exude light and energy wherever you go. Your father knew that. Your siblings know that. They know you don't need them. They know you don't necessarily need anyone."

Lena could feel her heart pounding at Eli's words. He'd figured out how to strip down all her walls, leaving her emotionally naked. Lena got up to hide her tears.

"Unless I'm wrong, of course."

This time, it was Eli that got up and moved directly behind Lena so that he could feel the warmth of her red hair radiate to his lips.

Lena didn't turn around. She just turned her head halfway and asked, "What do you mean?"

Eli gently turned her toward him and put his hand on her cheek.

Slowly he put his face right next to hers and whispered his next question. His lips were so close to hers that it caused her to instinctively close her eyes. His warm breath was on her cheek and she held her own breath for a moment. She could hear the whispered words as plain as day.

"Lena. Is it true that you do not need a soul in this whole world? Are you destined to tackle life alone? Or ... can those walls come down? Maybe if only for me?"

Lena opened her eyes and looked up into his big, turquoise, searching eyes that she had grown to love. Suddenly, those eyes were just hers and looking at only her. The moment she had dreamed about so many times was happening and time stood still. She could feel his thumb caress her jawline.

She could only softly let out his name. That was all she could muster. "Eli ..."

At that moment, Eli pulled her chin toward him, so her lips reached his. Then, he slowly kissed Lena in a way that made her feel like she was going to melt right there. Just one small, gentle, feathery kiss was all it took. He pulled back, not removing his hands from her face but looking deeply into her eyes for her reaction. She wrapped her arms around him to steady herself. His lips were so soft but so strong. He put her into a trance, and she could not snap out of it.

Eli whispered slow and soft again, so only she could hear. "I've imagined doing that so many times in my head. In so many ways, in so many places, at so many different times."

Lena looked at him with sleepy eyes. She was still drunk on his kiss. "Why now?"

Eli looked at her with a mischievous grin she had never seen before. "I could no longer resist you."

Lena's grin was mischievous as well. "I hope it lived up to your expectations."

Eli pulled Lena into his broad chest. "It certainly did." He hugged her, then looked into her eyes again. "Of course, if you'd like to make sure ..."

Eli kissed her yet again, but this time his kiss held more need and passion. Eli was no longer worried about crossing lines; he was breaking down walls. Lena had never felt so happy in her entire life.

CHAPTER *12*

Eli and Lena rode happily back to the ranch. This time, Lena felt seventeen again, and Eli was grinning like a schoolboy. When they arrived, Allie was waiting.

"Lena, there's trouble."

Of course, there was. Wasn't there always? "I haven't even been gone that long!"

Allie looked panicked. "You will want to head for the house right away."

Lena and Eli both dismounted their horses. They tied them to the barn and started for the house.

Allie stopped Eli and looked at him apologetically. "Um, Eli. Maybe you should put the horses away?"

Eli nodded slowly. He understood. This was family-only business, but he looked questioningly at Lena anyways. It was suddenly hard for them to be away from each other. Although their relationship was blossoming, the family functions were not yet a united affair.

"I'll be okay, Eli."

He nodded cautiously. Their hearts were attached now and there was a need to protect her.

Lena looked over her shoulder once more to give Eli a reassuring smile, then reluctantly went into the farmhouse to find everyone in there, along with Hunter.

"What's going on?" Lena asked.

It was Lois that spoke next. It was obvious that she was losing patience. She spat her words on the table. "Okay, Hunter. Everyone is here. What do you need to tell us?"

Hunter, a nervous wreck, was wringing his hands. "No, not everyone."

Galen was losing his patience. "For crying out loud, Hunter. Let's get on with this!"

Just then, William walked in nonchalantly. It was obvious he had no idea there was drama. He began to look around, baffled.

"Okay. *Now*, everyone is here."

William slowly found a seat. It was obvious that he'd had no plans to stay originally. "Uh, what's going on?"

Everyone but Hunter started to look at each other, searching for clues in each other's faces. Hunter just looked down, as if he were searching for words. Allie slipped into the last remaining chair.

Hunter looked up, as if he had come up with some nerve from deep within himself. "I'll get right to the point. I want my share of the Maleno legacy."

A loud silence filled the room. Lena could suddenly hear every tick from the clock on the wall. Everyone just sat in their chair, waiting for the punchline of some weird, twisted joke none of them understood.

It was Gracie that broke the silence. "What in the hell are you talking about? You are the help. I mean, fine as you are, you are still the help."

Charlotte responded to Gracie's initial argument. "I mean, if you're proposing, I will certainly think about it. You're definitely easy on the eyes."

Hunter became exasperated. The twins had a way of breaking the best concentration. "What? No!"

Slamming her hands on the table, Lena rose.

"Spit it out, Hunter. I've had enough surprises for the past few weeks, and I've certainly had enough of having my life flipped upside down for the past few months. If you've got something to say, then spit it out. Otherwise, I'm going to bed. I am way out of patience for playing games."

Hunter looked her in the eye, and Lena knew something was up. "Sit down, Lena. Is that any way to talk to your brother?"

She stared down Hunter, who met her challenge. Suddenly feeling her chest tightening, she went to the drawer for her inhaler.

After she calmed down, she talked in a low, slow voice. Everyone else just watched, afraid to speak. "What are you talking about?"

Hunter looked around until he found William. "Want to tell them, William?"

William, sitting on a heater in the back of the kitchen, was just as puzzled as anyone. "Tell who, what? I don't even know what the hell you are talking about!"

Hunter sighed. "You people make me tired. Okay. Years ago, William, you had an affair. Well, more than one, to be honest. You lost your wife. You ran into the arms of Lois Maleno, who was terribly upset at her husband for putting a lien on the ranch for settling some gambling debts, no?"

Lois' face turned bright red this time. Lena had never seen her look so ashamed in her life. She just wanted to melt into the linoleum.

"The result was a daughter. Am I wrong, Helena? Mr. Maleno adopted yet another Maleno daughter. The only true Maleno is you, Galen."

Gracie decided to take pure advantage of the situation. "Well, well, well. Lena, your ass isn't made of gold after all now, is it!"

Charlotte followed. "Imagine you being as low as the rest of us! Not a blood Maleno!"

Lena began to rise from her seat, feeling like she was going to hurl. Surely, there was somewhere she could run. Lois put her arm in front of her, blocking her path.

Lois stood up this time and yelled through her tears, "Enough! Knock it off. You are all Malenos!"

Hunter continued, a renewed confidence in his tone. "And, since Mr. Maleno took care of William's children, I would have been in the will like you all, had he known."

Although tears ran down her cheeks, Lois was strong. She was a mama bear with her cubs, and she was not going to allow Hunter to strong-arm her family. "No. You are not my child, Hunter. This is not going to work."

"Technicality, Mrs. Maleno." Hunter thought he would have felt prouder of himself. The plan his mother had worked out should have felt much better, in his opinion. Suddenly, he wanted to turn back time. He was doing this because he was in a vulnerable place. He chose to act despicable because he thought it showed the confidence that he was searching for to pull this off.

William, who seemed dazed, stood up and rushed to the table. "Wait. You are the son of …" His voice trailed off as if he was putting together the pieces of the puzzle.

Hunter looked hopeful. "Yes. Isabella Maleno. My mother is your aunt, Helena, and I am your half brother."

Everyone sat in stunned silence for a few seconds. Galen was the first to come to grips with everything. "Did your adopted mother know this when she came to my law firm to establish her will?"

Hunter looked ashamed. "Yes. It was her plan all along." Hunter's confidence was waning. He had to pull it together before everyone put the pieces together. Galen already had a look in his eye that claimed suspicion. Hunter predicted that he knew there was more to the story. His mother had become Galen's client to gain information. But Hunter was always worried that would give Galen a license to fish for information just as easily.

A piece of paper that Hunter produced made its way onto the table. Galen picked it up cautiously and read it. After reading it, Galen dropped the paper, stood up, and began pacing the kitchen. The sisters began to pass the paper around the table, reading it one by one.

"You can see that the injunction reads that I want 15 percent of your Maleno inheritances."

Lena's head was spinning. How could she experience heaven and hell in the same day?

CHAPTER *13*

"No." Lena just sat there and said the word softly. It was like she was in shock.

"There isn't an option for 'no.' Isabella is Lorenzo's only surviving relative. Ren inherited this estate from their parents because Isabella is estranged from the family. It's all legal."

Lois looked up at Hunter. "Well. You certainly double-crossed us all, didn't you?"

Hunter looked sadly at Lois. "Lois, that honestly was not my intention. I hope you can believe that." He felt himself shrinking. *Confident! Stop being wishy-washy,* he could hear his mother say.

Allie, incapable of believing such a conniver could be in their midst, was having a hard time keeping up with this whole thing. "Wait. So, you are not only our cousin but our brother?"

It was Lena that butted in. "No, that honor is all mine, Allison." Allie was still confused but decided not to say anything.

Galen had another question for Hunter. "Why was your mother estranged from the family?"

Hunter looked daggers at William. "That would be because of daddy dearest over there. When my mother cheated on her husband with William and became pregnant with her only child, that didn't sit well with her husband. He left her and took every cent. My grandparents were supposedly so ashamed that they threw both of us out on the street. My mother had to fight for everything she had. She had too much pride to ask her brother for help. She wouldn't ask you, either, William. She just devised a plan to someday get her share of the estate that she deserved."

Almost not realizing she was saying it out loud, Allie said, "That's why Daddy adopted us."

Gracie looked at her, astonished. "What?"

Allie looked at her sister. "Don't you see? Losing his sister obviously hurt Daddy dearly. He would never let that happen again, so he adopted us. Mama, did he know about Lena?"

Lois looked down, nodded her head affirmatively, and began to cry again.

Galen turned from his pacing and pointed to his mother. "You mean he *knew*? My father allowed William to stay?" William looked down.

"I don't believe this!" Galen threw up his hands in outrage. "Lena, please don't tell me *you* knew!"

Lena looked at Galen. "It was responsible for my last hospital visit."

Galen suddenly looked like a light bulb went on in his head. "Oh I see."

Lena could feel the room spinning. "I need some air."

Galen moved in front of her. "We aren't finished with this."

Outraged, Lena turned to her entire family. "So, anyone else here find out days ago that the person who brought you up isn't really your biological father but rather the ranch hand that was on the ranch your entire childhood? No? How about any of you find out that your mama had an affair and you were the result? No? Last question. Anyone find out that their cousin is their brother because their real father had two affairs, one with their mother and one with their aunt, and their long-lost brother is trying to take some of your inheritance away? Again? No takers?"

Even Charlotte and Grace just looked at each other in silence.

"Galen? You are the product of our mother and the man we all believed was our father. So, how about you take your declarations, move out of my way, and let me out of here before you regret it?"

Galen suddenly looked heartbroken for Lena. He slowly moved away and allowed her to pass.

Lena hastily moved for the door. Once it opened, she bolted across the porch and down the steps, into someone's unexpected arms.

Eli. In all his brilliance and beauty, he was there. She was falling, and he was catching her.

"Eli! What are you doing here?"

Eli just smoothed back her hair. In the sweetest voice she'd ever heard, he said, "Ya know, you folks need to keep those windows closed. Folks are bound to eavesdrop." Then, he kissed her cheek sweetly.

Lena was so relieved that she didn't have to tell him the entire story. "You heard about my new cousin-brother, did ya?" she said as she tried to laugh through the tears.

Eli just shook his head. He took her hand and stroked it gently. "You got some better shoes besides those slippers?

Lena looked quizzically at him. "I have some boots in the barn. Would that do?"

"Perfect. I'm thinking we might head up to Willow Rose tonight. Unless you'd rather stay to find out if Gale is your long-lost grandpa ..."

"No, thanks. I'm going for the boots right now."

Eli laughed. "I'm heading for the truck."

Lena ran to the barn, retrieved her old boots, and met Eli at his truck.

They were silent for about a mile. Eli had decided to take the long way around.

"I have an idea." Eli was full of ideas today. "I've got some rules."

Lena scrunched up her nose. "Rules?"

Eli scrunched back at her. "Rules. From now till sunup, there will be no talk of who's related to who."

"I'm liking your rules so far."

Eli thoughtfully proceeded. "There will be no talk of the recently departed."

"Another good rule."

"No discussion of relatives that have recently moved in."

"Love it."

"And there will be no talk of anyone employed on this ranch."

"What's left to talk about?"

Eli laughed. "Absolutely everything else."

"Then pull over."

Eli looked at her, shocked. "Huh?"

Lena looked at him, totally serious. "You heard me. Pull over."

Eli suddenly looked frightened. "Lena, I'm sorry if I offended you."

Lena's voice was more determined. "Pull. Over. Eli."

Eli could feel his palms sweat. That had totally backfired. He pulled over, not knowing what he had done wrong.

Much to his dismay, he found that Lena had kicked off her boots and had let her hair down. Lena tried her best not to grin at that face. It was "the" face. The face Eli always made when she let her hair down. It made her feel sexy and edgy.

Lena climbed over to Eli and straddled him until they were now nose to nose.

"You did not offend me. I want to talk about the kiss we shared the other day." Lena wrapped her hands around his neck and laced her fingers together. Then, she put her forehead on his.

Eli could feel his blood pressure come back to normal. He laughed flirtatiously.

"Ohhhhhhh. That kiss. Hmmmm ... I'm trying really hard to remember ..."

Lena just put her head down on his shoulder. "You are not going to do this to me, are you?"

Eli just smiled and pulled her lips to his and passionately kissed her. He could feel her body start to warm to his touch.

"You mean that kiss?"

Lena just closed her eyes. "Yes. That's the one. I want more, Eli. And not because this time in my life sucks right now or because you are the best thing in my life. I'm done admiring you from my bedroom window like I have for months."

Eli pretended to have a look of shock on his face. "What? You admired me from ..."

Lena just looked at him. "Eli. Really." Eli just laughed and Lena continued her sentiment. "I want to share every part of myself with you. I want you to know me. To feel me. To ..." Lena stopped. She moved her lips, but the words were stuck.

Eli put his finger to her lips and whispered, "To ... what?" Lena looked down. "Never mind."

Lena started to climb off Eli, but he gently coaxed her back. He pulled a stray strand of hair between his fingers and started to twirl it around. His next phrase was a whisper.

"To … love you? Was that what you were going to say?"

Eli's turquoise eyes were bigger than ever. His hair had curled on his forehead and his lips were pink and swollen from having kissed her so passionately. His hands were so gentle as they rubbed her back. Lena was attracted to his bravery, to be able to say something like that. She shook her head, telling herself that she must have forced him to say such a thing.

"Oh, Eli. I didn't mean to—"

Eli stopped her again. "Let me show you how much I love you, Lena."

After a kiss that made her weak in the knees, Eli started the truck again and proceeded to Willow Rose. They headed off to the river, slept under a blanket of stars, and enjoyed showing their love for each other all night long.

CHAPTER *14*

Lena could feel the sun coming up on her face. She lazily turned to her side and pinched herself, wondering if she had been dreaming. She had woken up numerous times and just smiled to herself as she lay on Eli's chest, watching it rise and fall. She felt the cool, dewy air rest on the blanket that covered them, and the cicadas that had sung them to sleep. The rustle of the water was calming, and the stars were breathtaking. She truly thought that this was what heaven was going to be like.

Now, Eli was already dressed, which Lena thought was a shame. He had built a fire, brewed some coffee, and made breakfast over the fire with things she figured he had in the back of his truck. Lena was blissfully exhausted.

"That smells terrific!"

Eli turned to look at her. He thought she looked like a goddess, with her hair all disheveled and wild. "Good morning, my love."

Lena could feel her cheeks blush and she looked away shyly. She didn't know if she would ever get used to hearing such terms of endearment, but she was certainly going to try.

Eli approached Lena with a plate of food, coffee, and a steamy kiss.

"Why, Eli Miller! Did you have plans to seduce me this whole time?"

Eli looked at her, shocked. "What are you talking about?"

Lena wrapped the blanket around her and joined Eli. "Food ... a blanket ... coffee pot ... wood for a fire ... Eli, come on." She teased him as he flushed crimson.

"Okay, so maybe I ran home really fast during that family meeting and put a few things together ... but, I swear, Lena. I really didn't plan on ..."

Lena interrupted him as she put a finger to his lips. "Hey. Eli. Honey, I know. I'm just teasing you. You are a great man, with the best of intentions. I know you did not come up here to use me. You could never do that. I would imagine your intention was just to talk all night, maybe just cuddle in your truck?"

Eli looked at her gratefully. "Thank you for understanding that. No, I expected to cuddle by the river. Making love as we did was truly not my intention. I don't regret it though."

Lena smiled. She picked at the food on her plate, then looked thoughtfully at Eli. "So, what does this all mean, Eli?"

Eli looked back at her, confused. "What does what mean?"

"This. Us."

Eli moved closer to Lena and put her plate of food down. He took her hands in his and looked in her eyes.

"Lena, I had a childhood that didn't suit my heart. Speak only when spoken to. Never show anger. Okay, that was a good rule to live by. My parents were extraordinary people. But my heart did not fit that lifestyle."

Lena looked at him and tilted her head. That had to be so painful. "I'm so sorry, Eli."

"I'm not. I learned so many good things growing up Amish. I would not give up my childhood experiences for anything. It made me who I am today. And, I would be lying if I said I didn't miss it.

"But, as I grew, I realized it wasn't for me. I was always longing for more. I was always dreaming. It wasn't fair to me, and it certainly wasn't fair to the Amish. I could never be what they wanted me to be. That was not the lifestyle I wanted, Lena.

"The man my parents raised. The values my parents gave me. That's the man I want to be. It's the man I am. Your sister tried to change me. I found out that I don't want to change. I want someone who will accept every part of me. Someone who will accept who I used to be and the person I am now."

Lena looked at him and stroked his hair. "Eli, are you sure that person is me?"

Eli put his hand on her cheek. "Oh, Lena. When your sister and I started a relationship, she stepped into a new world like me. It was about timing for us. She had just come home from that fancy school and didn't know where to go next. I was in the same place. We had very long talks about that. Deep talks I'm sure she will never admit.

"I loved the Charlie that was deep and honest. But that Charlie rarely came out very often, and never for more than just me. The Charlie that ruled her heart was manipulative and calculating. I am not the man to break down the walls she needs torn down."

Lena nodded. "Manipulative and calculating. That's the one I know."

"There's another side to her, Lena. I wish she'd show it to you."

Lena looked down sadly. "Do you still love her, Eli?" Lena could feel herself holding back tears as she asked the question.

Eli pulled the blanket off Lena and pulled her close to him. He pulled her chin up so her lips met his and kissed her with such gentleness, she feared all strength would leave her body.

"I believe it's impossible for your heart to completely stop loving someone. There will always be a small corner of my heart that loves that honest side of your sister. I only loved that part of her. You can't be in love with just one part of a person. I'm desperately in love with you, Lena. I'm in love with every single inch of you. I have been for such a long time. I'm drawn to you by this invisible force and there's no stopping it. I won't hide it any longer, Lena."

Eli picked her up and carried her over to their makeshift bed, made of an old comforter Eli had brought. He laid Lena down while Lena unbuttoned his shirt. She wanted him one more time before returning to her chaotic life and Eli was not about to argue.

As they were watching the sunrise together under a blanket, a sound broke their silence.

"Really? Are you serious? I have been working so hard to push Dirk and Allie together. It was you I had to worry about all this time, Eli?"

Lena and Eli both turned their heads around to see a very angry Derek looking at them. Lena wanted just one whole day without a complication in her life.

CHAPTER *15*

The words startled them both. Eli pulled Lena close to him, protectively, while Lena flushed four different shades of red.

"Oh for God's sake, put some clothes on. I'll turn around."

An irritated Derek turned around as Lena and Eli exchanged worried and embarrassed glances. Clothes began flying back and forth as the couple dressed.

As Lena and Eli began putting socks and boots on, Eli informed Derek that it was clear for him to turn around. Eli still hovered protectively over Lena. He trusted no one, and he was defensive because of how Derek was acting.

"How long has this been going on?" an irritated Derek asked. It was noticeably clear that he could barely contain his anger or sarcasm. The more irritated Derek became, the more defensive Eli grew.

Lena began to grow irritated. "Since when do I owe you any explanations about my life, Derek Hopstef? That means love life or any other."

Derek was getting angrier by the second. Pacing, he balled his fists by his sides. His face was growing red, and there was a vein popping out of his neck. "Oh really! Who has been there through everything? ME! That's who! Who has slept in barns for you? Me! This guy was with your sister! Dirk has barely been here a minute. Besides, he is now with your other sister. I'm the only true person you can depend on! You are mine!"

The way Derek talked about Lena being his property infuriated Eli. *He's young, Eli. He's never been in love before. He probably hasn't had much of a father figure. Don't allow him to cause you rage. That's not the way.* Eli let out a slow, therapeutic breath and talked slowly and calmly, both for his and Derek's well-being. "That will be quite enough, Derek. That's not how love works, son. You don't get a piece of property. Love isn't a game of Monopoly."

Derek turned around and put his finger in Eli's chest. "Don't. Call. Me. Son."

Derek pulled back a fist and almost hurled it at Eli when Lena jumped in between. In a split second, Eli's whole world flashed. Lena put her hand on Eli's chest. The gesture was to calm him and tell him to just relax.

"Get out of my way, Lena! It's time for me to show him that I'm a man, too!"

Lena tried to plead with him. "Derek, this is not how you show everyone who you are! I don't love you. I love Eli."

Derek slowly lowered his fist. Lena's words had cut him to the core. Derek swallowed hard, trying not to show that her words had any effect. Eli stayed close to Lena. He was not going to allow Derek within one hundred feet of her.

Gathering as much of his dignity as he could, Derek spoke to Lena in a soft voice. He tried to take her by the hand, but Eli pulled her back. Derek looked at him with sad eyes but gave up on trying to take her hand. Instead, he just pleaded with her. "You never gave me a chance, Lena. I knew you were interested in Dirk the day he was at your fire. Why don't I get a chance?"

Lena and Eli suddenly felt bad for Derek. It was the first time he'd loved anyone, and he had fallen hard.

Lena moved over toward Derek and touched his arm. "Derek, I'm truly sorry. Love is not an audition. It's a calling. And, my heart is called to Eli. It always will be."

Eli moved toward him as well. "Derek, nothing is going to tear us apart."

Derek pulled away quickly and yanked his arm from Lena's grasp. "Bull. You've been in love for five minutes. You are just ignoring me, Lena! I know that you read romance novels to put you to sleep at night. I know you tell everyone your favorite food is steak, but it's actually mint chocolate chip ice cream. I know you get on a horse to ride whenever you feel claustrophobic, even though you never take your inhaler."

Lena was both afraid and sad. It was killing her that she had to hurt him this way. "Oh, Derek. You are such a kind soul. And I value your friendship. But. I. Don't ..."

She stopped. Not only was the look in Derek's eyes more than she could bear, but he began yelling over her, mid-sentence.

"No! Don't say it. You just never gave me a chance! Dammit, Eli! You got in my way!" He quickly shoved Lena out of the way, causing her to fall to the dirt and onto her arm. As Lena screamed in pain, Eli charged toward her.

Eli tried to reach Lena, but Derek surprisingly grabbed him by the collar, spun him around, and caught him off guard. Derek delivered a blow to Eli's jaw that caused the corner of his mouth to bleed. Eli staggered but refused to fall. He defensively returned the blow to Derek, causing him to fall hard in the dirt. Eli lunged, turned him around, and pulled his arm behind his back, pinning him into the dirt. Before letting him back up, Eli tried to reason with him.

"I didn't want to do that, *man*, but you have to be willing to learn before you can lead. Lena needs a man willing to lead. You need to learn to follow first, Derek."

Eli waited a few seconds, then allowed a stunned, humbled, and embarrassed Derek to stand. He was not expecting humble Eli to best him. Deep down, he knew that Eli could take him if needed. He just never thought Eli had the heart to do so. He had underestimated how tough Eli was.

When Derek stood, he was dirty and dusty, and his cheek was beginning to bruise. Eli had tackled him near his truck and the grass was still wet from the dew.

Eli wiped the blood from his lip. While moving toward Lena, he still tried to reason with Derek. "Being young doesn't make you weak, Derek. That mouth of yours makes you weak. You aren't willing to learn. You want respect because you tell people you should have it. Respect is earned. Usually without saying much, *son*." He spat out the word *son* as a sign of disrespect, knowing that Derek would perceive it as an attack on his age.

Neither Lena nor Derek expected the sarcasm in Eli's voice. Lena discovered that Eli used sarcasm to hide his true anger.

Derek stayed silent, turned around, and headed back for the ranch.

Eli turned toward Lena, who was wiping tears from her eyes. For a woman who never cried, she seemed to be doing a lot of that lately.

"I didn't think it was possible to be more in love with you, Eli. After that, I definitely am!"

Eli kissed her lips and pulled her tight. There was a little caution flag in his head that was waving. He didn't like the situation with Derek Hopstef. He did not like it one bit.

CHAPTER *16*

"Lena, are you okay?" Eli carefully pulled Lena up from where she had fallen. She was nursing her wrist.

"Yes, Eli. I'm fine. I hurt this wrist falling from a horse a while back. It really can't be broken. It just hurts if I knock it around. I promise I'm fine."

Lena and Eli packed up the truck and headed for the ranch. It took about an hour after their encounter with Derek, but they found ways to lighten the mood. Soon they forgot all about Derek Hopstef and the gloom lifted from their morning. Their brunch conversation was easy and fun. They talked about life and the future and their dreams. Lena wanted this carefree mood to last forever. Then, something caught her eye. Eli slowed down.

"Well, hey there! What are you two doing?" Eli smiled at the two people looking in the window, trying to get a glimpse at the passenger.

Dirk suddenly had a sly look on his face. "Galen wants Zars ready to race next month. Allie and I have made it our project."

Eli ignored the obvious silly grins on their faces. "Have you found a jockey yet?"

Dirk and Allie looked nervous. Eli and Lena glanced suspiciously at each other. Lena couldn't put her finger on it, but her instincts told her to be wary.

Allie drew out her response. "We … have …" Allie kicked a rock with her foot. Lena was growing impatient. What was she missing?

Lena leaned up in the seat. "So?"

As Dirk and Allie looked nervously at each other again, Lena put the pieces together and barreled out of the truck. *"Allison Hope Maleno, you can't be serious!"*

Eli finally caught up and started out of the truck. He fiddled with the seat belt frantically until he finally was able to shut the door. Allie smiled at the scene, even though she knew that Eli was trying to be intense.

"Dirk! I thought you had more sense than this! What are you doing?"

Eli soon realized that his hands were on Dirk's biceps and he was shaking him. Now it was Lena that laughed. Dirk was a good head taller than Eli and about six inches broader. Although Eli was a strong-looking man, he looked incredibly small in comparison to Dirk. He could certainly hold his own, and if the circumstances arose, Eli would give him a run for his money. But in the end, Dirk would clean up against Eli.

Dirk just brushed Eli's hands off him as if he were chasing away a mosquito. "Look. You guys *must* see her ride! Lena, you aren't the only one who has a sixth sense about horses!"

Allie suddenly started to talk insistently. Lena got the impression that Allie had been rehearsing this speech. "There have only been six women jockeys at the Kentucky Derby. Six! Come on, Lena. It'll be easy for me to make weight! And Zars loves me!"

Feeling protective over both Maleno women, Eli began to pace. He stopped as he looked at Dirk to ask his next question, considering whether he could trust Dirk's judgment anymore. "Has Galen heard about this?"

Dirk and Allie both looked down at the same time, as if they had been reprimanded for stealing someone's toy in kindergarten. Allie looked up for a moment, considered a reply, but looked back down and played with the rock again.

Lena looked down into Allie's eyes, even though she was looking down. Lena was grasping at hope, praying someone in the family knew about this scheme. "Mother?"

No answer. Horrified, Lena turned from Allie and looked at Eli.

Eli took his cue from Lena and hoped that maybe Dirk had talked this over with someone. "William?"

Dirk suddenly looked up and attempted to reason with Eli. It was obvious this plan was solely between the two of them and had not been thought out with anyone else. "Look. Our plan was to put Allie up there, undetected, and show everyone how well she rides. No one will be able to resist ..."

Dirk's sentence trailed off when he looked at Lena's explosive body language. Her foot began to tap uncontrollably as her arms crossed in front of her body. Eli was pacing again, and his hand raked his hair nervously.

"I see. Put everyone in a 'can't take no for an answer' situation?"

Dirk looked up sheepishly at Lena. "Well ..."

His long, drawn-out answer infuriated Lena. She looked at Eli. "This is crazy!"

This time, it was Allie that was growing restless. She ran over to Lena, uncrossed her sister's arms, and took Lena's hands in her own. "Please, Lena. You know I've never truly fit in. I'm not a fighter like my sisters. I've never had your fire, Lena. I've never had Charlie's wit. I've never had Gracie's courage. I've been the 'good' one. The patient one. The predictable one. The safe one."

Lena could feel her heart soften. That was all true, but one of them had to be that person. One of the sisters had to be the sensible and sweet one. Lena thought it was Allie's greatest strength and wondered why she considered that a flaw.

"Lena, when I'm on that horse, courage just comes over me. I can feel the fire in my soul. I am the one everyone is watching." Allie's eyes were glimmering and bright. Her hands were open, and her face told Lena that Allie had found her true calling. Still, Lena thought she had to try once more to talk her out of this insane plan.

"Allie, you could get hurt!"

"And one spook from an animal on a trail ride can't get you hurt?"

Damn. Allie had her there. A rattler had scared Myrna during a trail ride last August. Myrna had reared up, dumping Lena beside the rattler. Myrna then continued to stomp the rattler, stomping Lena's arm in the process. Lena now sported a rod in her left arm, which was throbbing as they spoke.

"I ..." Lena had nothing else to say.

Dirk knew they had her, and he moved in on his opportunity. "Please. Keep this quiet until you see her ride. If you say no with everyone else, then okay. Just give her a chance."

Eli and Lena looked at each other with caution.

"I don't know." Eli still wasn't convinced.

Dirk took the lead this time. "I promise. Every morsel of her safety is in my hands. And ..."

Dirk looked at Allie and brushed a hand across her cheek.

"Lena. Eli. I love her. If anything happened to her, I would die." Although Dirk was saying this to Lena and Eli, his eyes never left Allie's.

Allie had tears in her eyes. This was obviously the first time she had heard Dirk admit such a thing. Lena chuckled to herself. Tall, burly Dirk and petite, tiny Allie. Instinctively, Lena felt she could trust this.

Allie burst off the road and into Dirk's arms. Her arms went around his neck and her legs wound around his waist, holding him tightly. "Oh, Dirk. I love you too! I love you so much, you could never ever know! I can't believe you just said that!" Then she lowered her face and started showering him with kisses.

Eli laughed out loud. "Okay, you two. Get a room."

Dirk put Allie down. "Don't you mean a spot by the river?"

Lena's mouth dropped open. "Allison Hope!"

Dirk just laughed. "Although I'm a little worried about young Derek, we all chuckled to ourselves, imagining the scene he walked in on."

Eli and Lena both flushed crimson.

Lena tried to change the subject. "Enough about that. If anything, and I mean *anything* happens on the day of this 'test run,' it's a no. Got it?"

Allie jumped into Lena's arms this time. "Yes! Yes! Oh thank you, Lena!"

Dirk just looked at Eli, who was obviously still unsure. "Eli?"

Eli reluctantly looked at Lena and sighed. "Ugh. I guess I better make sure that horse is in the best condition. I'll be watching over you and this horse. Lena will be watching over Allie. Deal?"

Dirk smiled and stuck out his hand. "Deal!"

The two men shook as Allie and Lena stood with their arms around each other. Lena hoped this was not the creation of yet another nightmare.

CHAPTER 17

Lena had been able to avoid most of her family for most of the day. She had a long trail ride of Girl Scouts that had been successful. Allie's situation was stressful, but it also made her smile as well. She was glad to finally see some Maleno fire in Allie and for her to find her own way. Lena hoped that spending more time with Dirk would keep Allie away from Gracie and Charlie.

She tried to avoid squaring off with Hunter or William, clueless of how to start a conversation with her mother, and missed Galen. After Daddy died, it had been just Lena and Galen for months.

As if her thoughts produced him out of midair, she heard a rustle of footsteps in the barn and there he was. She noticed how Galen had aged since Daddy died. But he was still just as dashing.

When Galen walked in, she noticed how much closer to normal he looked. His hair was a little more salt and pepper every time she looked at it, which reminded her of her daddy. Tall and lanky, Galen was stately looking. He was in a pair of dark denim, well-fitted jeans, a tight royal blue V-neck T-shirt, and a looser-fitting flannel with the sleeves rolled up. He was wearing a pair of boat shoes with no socks. Daddy had always yelled at him for that. He thought it was senseless to be on a ranch with no socks.

There was no expensive lawyer watch on his wrist. No leather belt around his jeans, and no silk tie around his neck. He was just Galen.

"You out of the office so early?"

Galen smiled. "Well, besides the fact that I miss you, we have a lot to discuss. Come to dinner with your only, yet super attractive, brother?"

Lena rolled her eyes, then giggled. "What about everyone else?"

Galen giggled back. "Mother and the twins have taken a trip to New York City. They thought the break would do everyone good. Allie wanted to stay. I think she and Dirk have a thing."

Lena smiled. "They do. It's more than a thing. They are in love."

Galen looked surprised. "Already?"

Lena shrugged. "You can't stand in the way of true love, Galen." She noticed that Galen became withdrawn at that comment.

Galen continued. "I sent Eli to town to pick up some supplies for me. William and Hunter have been spending evenings together. He seems to be settling Hunter down. And Derek? Well, we will leave that to dinner conversation."

Lena suddenly felt giddy. Dinner with Galen? She'd missed him so much. "Okay, Gale! I will go to dinner with you. Casual?"

"Crab Shack?"

Lena licked her lips. "Yum."

Gale smiled. "An hour?"

"An hour."

Both siblings walked into the house to get ready. Lena pulled on a pair of blue jeans, boots, and a tank top. She pulled her hair into two low ponytails, her daddy's favorite. Gale just took off his flannel. He had on his tight blue V-neck and jeans. He changed his boat shoes to a pair of loafers. Lena never understood why Galen was single. Any woman would be lucky to have him. He was often uptight, but he had a lot of responsibility!

"Ready?" Gale was sitting in a recliner, reading the paper as Lena came downstairs. If that didn't look like Daddy, she didn't know what did. Now he was even mirroring his mannerisms!

"Sure am!"

The ride in the car was fun. Gale told her of her sisters' antics. Lena had forgotten how much she missed his sarcasm.

When they got to the Crab Shack, they ordered their usual and Galen began to speak.

"I feel like I should just lay things out one by one, Lena. I don't want you to feel defensive with me. Both of our worlds have been turned upside down and we have been trying to hide instead of helping each other. Daddy would tan our hides for such behavior."

Lena chuckled at Gale's mix of Daddy's whoop-ass terminology and sophisticated language.

"I'm ready." She braced herself. Galen was a very shoot-from-the-hip kind of guy. He didn't sugarcoat anything. It was one of the features Lena loved and hated about him the most.

"Let's start with Derek. I let him go today."

Lena almost spat out the water she was drinking. "You what?" She couldn't believe her ears! Derek was vital to the ranch. It was going to be very hard to replace him.

Galen was prepared for that response from her. He was already in lawyer mode, defending his decision. "Lena. When he came down from that hill today, he told me what happened. He also told me a lot more."

Lena furrowed her brow. She didn't care what he told Galen. All she cared about was the ranch, and this was going to hurt the place terribly. "Like what, Galen? What could he have possibly told you that warranted firing one of our hardest workers? Do you know what it's going to be like to replace him?"

Galen sat back in his chair as if he were sitting on a great piece of evidence. He paused dramatically before he remarked, "The password to unlock your phone is Ginger28." He tapped the table, sat back in the chair, and looked proud of himself as he said it.

Lena's eyes grew wide and her mouth dropped open. "How did you ..." Her voice trailed off.

Galen finally knew he had her right where he wanted her. He sat back in his seat and took her hand across the table. Things were going to get hard, and he wanted her to have the support of a brother now, not a lawyer.

"There's more, Lena." Galen's big-brother voice, which Lena hated, was kicking in. Even though Galen was younger by only a year, he often took on the role of her big brother. Big-brother voice meant that something scary was under her bed or her high school boyfriend was a cheater or ... she looked away for a moment. Big-brother voice meant that the doctors had done everything they could, but Daddy was gone.

Lena looked back and Galen was looking at her with sympathetic eyes. "He's been ... stalking? Us?"

"Not us. Just you. In fact, he put himself in a place for Hunter to get information."

Lena pulled her hand away. "What? No. That can't be. He's odd, yes. But he would never hurt me that completely."

Derek was more than a ranch hand; he was also a friend. Lena genuinely cared about Derek, more than Galen realized.

"Lena, I don't mean to hurt you with what I have to say, but you must hear it. Hunter and Dirk live in the stable together. Hunter saw Dirk the night at your fire. He approached Derek about it, knowing how Derek felt about you."

Fire burned in Lena's eyes and Galen felt the urge to talk faster.

"Hunter told Derek he would push Dirk and Allie together if he would get him information. Although, I'm not sure anyone had to really work to push Dirk and Allie together."

Galen tried to laugh, but Lena just looked at him, fire continuing in her eyes.

"That's how Allie ended up at the fire that morning, I suppose?"

The look on his face gave her the answer she needed.

"I can't fire Hunter because of what's going on. So? Right now, I've taken to another ploy."

Lena looked at him suspiciously. "What's that?"

"Reeling him in."

Lena looked at him with uncertainty. "Reeling him in. I don't like the sound of that, Galen."

Galen pretended to look shocked. "You don't think I'm smarter than ole Hunter, Lena?"

"It's not that at all, Galen! I just think that …"

Galen just laughed. "Hear me out. I'm going to kill him with kindness. I told him if he's going to get my 15 percent, I must trust that he will be good for the ranch. He will learn how to work it."

Lena looked shocked again. "What? Why would you give him your 15 percent, Galen? That's insane!"

Galen just put his finger to his lips. "Hear me out now. Hunter was surprised, but so far it's working."

Lena just looked at him, disbelieving. "Really. He's been nothing but pleasant with you about this whole thing, then."

Galen sat for a minute, looking for the right words. He had to proceed with caution, knowing that Lena was broken by all of this. She had endured a complete change of identity.

"Lena, I don't think Hunter is a bad guy. Deep in his soul, he is a good man. He felt horrible when I fired Derek today. He begged me not to do it. He admitted that it was his fault."

Lena looked up from playing with the water in her glass. "I'm glad you fired him after all, Galen. He's becoming a liability. It's not only his heart that's gotten hurt, but it will soon be another physical altercation. It won't be long before someone will truly hurt him for real."

Galen looked at Lena with a sly smile. "Yeeesssss. Speaking of that … Eli?"

Lena could feel her cheeks blush. Sometimes she hated being a redhead. "W-What about him? You like him, don't you?"

"Apparently, not as much as you."

Lena shifted nervously in her chair. Then she remembered what Eli said. He wouldn't hide his feelings for her. Lena thought maybe it was time she abided by the same principle.

She spoke very quickly. "I love him, Gale. And he loves me."

Gale looked at her thoughtfully as he took her hand again. "You realize that he and I will be having the talk, right?"

Lena looked, horrified, at Galen. "What? What talk?" She suddenly narrowed her eyes at Galen, which made him chuckle.

"*The* talk. Where I inform him that if he hurts you, I will break both of his legs in six different places."

Lena looked at him, annoyed. "Oh, Galen, seriously. How archaic!"

Galen just shook his head. "Archaic or not, I'm your only brother. Don't mess with it, Lena. It's just how it is."

Lena rolled her eyes. It was so nice to have Gale back. She just smiled and smiled at him, until he suddenly went pale. He turned white when a beautiful, raven-haired woman with a darker complexion walked in.

Galen was suddenly sick with worry. "Are you ready? I'll ask for the check up front. Let's go."

He was practically pulling Lena from the table. "Galen! What's wrong?"

Galen stopped and looked at her with serious eyes. There was a dramatic, urgent look on his face. "Helena Joy, do you love me?"

The full name let Lena know that he was serious and not playing around anymore. "Of course, Galen! You are the best brother in the world."

"Then please help me get out of here and I will answer every question you have on the way home."

Lena picked up her purse and followed him, confused as ever.

CHAPTER *18*

Galen paid the bill and practically ran to the car. Lena used the restroom, then came sauntering out to a very annoyed Galen, who was tapping his finger on the steering wheel. She barely closed the door before Galen began backing out. Lena figured she would allow him to drive onto the highway before she spoke.

"So, should I just start probing you for answers, or do you want to offer up an explanation on your own?"

Galen looked at her and thought he'd try an excuse. "Uh, indigestion?"

Lena gave him an annoyed look. "Galen …"

Galen pulled over and turned off the ignition. The top was down on his convertible since he knew it was Lena's favorite way to ride. It was such a beautiful night. The stars were out, and Lena could see the tops of the trees and some of the small hills.

Galen seemed to get ahold of himself while Lena was admiring the scenery. "Okay. You've been after me to date for a long time."

"I have."

"And I did. I dated that girl that came into the bar. Her name is Catherine. She stomped on my heart, and that's really all I want to say about it."

Galen suspected Lena was going to require more of an explanation. Of all his sisters, it was his luck that Lena, the one who knew him best, had witnessed his reaction to Catherine.

"But Galen!"

Galen just sighed. He was right. That was not going to suffice. He'd had such a nice time with his sister that was long overdue. The thought of overshadowing that with a huge story about the terrible failure that was his love life made him wince.

"How about this? If you truly let me have the talk with Eli … with my unending promise to be nice … I will tell you all about Catherine. Details and all."

Lena mulled it over for a minute. Annoyed, she finally answered. "Okay. Fine. But you promise to be nice! I get to hear all about Catherine right after!"

Galen made a cross sign over his heart. "Cross my heart!"

They both smiled and continued home. Driving up to the ranch house, Galen and Lena could see a shadow on the porch. Galen parked and they walked to the porch together. They slowly approached a pacing Hunter.

"Evenin'."

As flatly as she could, Lena returned his salutation. "Hunter. To what do I owe the pleasure?" It was hard to ignore the obvious disdain in Lena's voice.

Galen whispered in her ear, "Be nice, please." Lena didn't know why Galen was even entertaining this heathen.

"I'm here about Derek."

Galen walked over to the table on the porch and pulled out two chairs, signaling them both to sit down. "We have discussed this, Hunter. Derek's dismissal is due to his own cognizance. He needs to get on with his own life." Lena smiled at Galen's lawyer terminology.

Hunter stood up and began pacing. "It's my cogni—It's my fault! My greed got in the way. My mother needs the money. She told me all about this. She is the mastermind behind all of this." Hunter paused for a moment to stop rambling. "I didn't want anyone to get hurt."

Lena suddenly felt a twinge of pity for him now, which made Galen's dinner argument more evident. Hunter wasn't devious. He was simply subject to the true mastermind behind this scheme.

"Hunter, it's more than what happened with you. There's more to this than you know."

"We promise. What's happened with you isn't the only reason I fired him."

Hunter came back and sat in his seat and bowed his head. Galen and Lena looked at each other with sympathetic glances.

Lena looked at Hunter and proceeded. "Derek has been stalking me. That is not okay."

Hunter slowly looked up and looked at Lena. "That's what I mean. I know all about that and I took full advantage. Even though we really need this money, I really do want to be your brother. I want to be a part of a family! But what kind of brother takes advantage of someone stalking his own sister? Who does that? I'm so messed up."

Lena looked at Hunter. "You know this is the absolute worst way to become part of a family, right?"

Hunter let out a nervous laugh. "I thought the same thing, but my mother thought that this was the only way. I should have stuck to my instincts."

After an awkward silence, Galen spoke. "Hunter, why do you need this money?"

Hunter looked down again. Barely audible, he whispered, "I screwed up. I am actually a huge screw-up." Hunter's embarrassment prevented him from making eye contact with Galen and Lena. He looked away and bit his lip, hoping they would stop asking for more information but knowing they wanted to know more.

Lena gave a cautious look to Gale. "I think you better start at the beginning."

Hunter stood up and went over to the porch railing. He leaned against it and courageously looked both Lena and Galen in the eye. Gale moved so he could better see Hunter.

"I always knew who my parents were. My mom would never allow me to see my dad, and I never understood why. I was never allowed to ask questions. She would cut me off or just leave the room."

Hunter paused to make sure Galen and Lena were both paying attention. Galen responded with "Okay" to assure him that they were all on the same page.

Hunter took a deep breath and continued his story, looking back and forth between the Maleno siblings. "When I was eighteen, I went to the track. I didn't have a lot of emotional support as a child. I never learned how to talk to anyone. My mother was always stoic, strong, and cold. She always told me I had to rise above, but she never told me why. My childhood was very confusing."

Lena looked at Hunter as if she knew what he was going to say. "You went to the track to spy on William, right?"

"And you. I just wanted to see who you both were. I wanted to figure out what 'rise above' meant. The more I watched, the more confused I became."

Lena let out a sigh, relieved to find out her suspicions were incorrect, until Hunter continued his story.

"Unfortunately, I also started to bet on the horses and acquired quite a bit of debt."

Galen and Lena both looked at each other again. They knew all too well how easy it was to get into that kind of debt as the ranch had almost fallen into debt several times.

Hunter was choked up and his next words were broken. "My mom bailed me out. We have been living in poverty. Now she's very sick. Ovarian cancer. And I can't pay."

Lena and Galen both looked despondent at the circumstances, but they understood the severity of Hunter's situation.

"I see." That was all Galen could muster for the moment.

Lena suddenly started to smile. "Hunter, that was very brave of you to tell us your entire story. Honestly. I wish you had done that originally."

Hunter looked relieved. "That was my original plan. My mother didn't have any faith in that plan. She always told me the Malenos were cold people, as were all the rich. She suggested I fight fire with fire. If I didn't, I would be laughed off the ranch."

Lena and Galen looked down at the table and allowed the words to sink in. She felt it unfair that her aunt had this perception of her family and regretted that she never had the opportunity to meet her and change her mind. The thing she regretted most was that Daddy died before Lena had learned about all of this. She wished he were here right now so that he could talk to Hunter.

Lena thought about what her father would do in this situation. A plan formed in her mind. "I have an idea. Come with me, both of you."

The two gentlemen followed Lena to the stables. Lena and Galen murmured ahead of Hunter as he lingered behind. They stopped at the far end of the stable.

"Hunter, if you accept the offer we are about to make, will you rescind your suit claiming your 15 percent of our siblings' inheritance?"

Hunter looked questioningly at them. "I'm listening."

It was Galen that answered. "I don't think you meant to hoodwink this family; I think you were coaxed into it. I'd like to give you another chance, just like my father was so famous for doing."

Lena's throat grew tighter and her eyes fluttered closed. She forced herself to smile and fought hard to push away the melancholy thoughts of missing her father as Galen put his hand on her shoulder, recognizing her sadness but proceeding with his thought. "If you rescind that offer, I will, in turn, forward you $10,000 to help your mother get started on whatever treatment she may need. You are a good employee and you know your way around horses. The check will be made out to your mom or a medical provider so that you are not tempted in any way to pull into a horse track. Will that be enough?"

Hunter had tears in his eyes. "I don't know what to say! That will be more than enough."

Lena interjected. This time she was giddy with excitement. "There's more." She was sure she looked ridiculous to an outsider, but she loved helping people and she rarely had the opportunity.

"This gelding is almost three years old and totally green. Since Daddy died, we only have the manpower for Thus Spake Zarathustra, especially with Derek gone."

Hunter's face began to light up. Galen began to smile.

"We want to give you this horse, minus what it would cost to board him."

Hunter could barely contain himself. "I. But. You." He stuttered in awe, which made Lena chuckle in delight.

Galen laughed as well. "You will race him under Maleno Stables until he wins enough for you to pay back the $10,000 and any other expenses you accrue. In addition, you'll pay your own jockey. You'll train the horse and feed him. We will start an expense account that you will pay back."

Hunter took a few minutes to think it through. Once he was sure he could form actual sentences, he tried to speak. "Once I pay back every penny, he's mine?"

Lena moved away from the stable door, inviting Hunter over to see his horse. "No questions asked. If you continue to keep him here, there will just be a boarding cost, which I plan on discounting for you."

Hunter had a nice smile, which Lena was sure she had never seen before. "This is incredible!"

Galen was still smiling as well. "I will have papers drawn up. This will rescind all your claims to my father's estate."

Hunter moved over to look at his horse. "Yes, sir!" He was paying no attention to Galen now, only to the beautiful horse in front of him.

Lena moved over to Hunter and softly put a hand on his shoulder. "You will truly be a part of our family!" Hunter looked at her and smiled as she patted him on the shoulder again and started to catch up to Galen.

As Galen was walking out of the barn, he turned back to address Hunter.

"Hunter?"

Hunter looked away from his horse and turned to Galen. "Yes?"

"If you get into gambling trouble, all bets are off. Snowglider comes back to us and you forfeit everything you have in him. That will be in the contract. I will not bail you out."

Hunter looked back at the magnificent horse in front of him. "I completely understand."

Galen nodded in understanding.

As Hunter entered Snowglider's stable, he poked his head out of the gate. "Hey. Guys?"

Gale and Lena turn around to see tears falling from Hunter's cheeks.

Hunter looked at them with true sincerity. "Nobody ever did anything like this for me before. Could I ... I mean ..."

Galen went back to the stable door. "Aw, come here, ya big lug." Lena ran over and joined in Hunter's first sibling hug.

For once, he felt like he belonged somewhere.

CHAPTER *19*

The rest of the week went beautifully. Lena stayed mostly with Eli in his small, yet cozy and simple apartment. Lena adored it and Eli loved having her there. Galen went back to his long hours at the office. Hunter and William worked with Snowglider and were forming a great relationship, making up for lost time. Hunter smiled more than anyone else on the ranch. William invited him to stay at his smaller ranch about five miles away.

Allie and Dirk worked with Zars every day until they were dead on their feet. Allie loved the feeling of working so hard you could barely move. Her muscles were so tired she could barely stand it. They collapsed into bed each night at the stable and were happy to be in each other's arms.

Lena thought she was in heaven. It was the happiest they had all been in a very long time.

Lena opened the door of the creaky old truck and bounded out. "I'm going to go into the house to see if I got any mail."

"Okay, sweetheart," Eli called back. She was never going to tire of being called sweetheart.

"Mother, I still can't believe we bought all this stuff! Where am I going to wear all of this?" Charlotte was holding about fifteen different-sized bags in her hands.

"Yes, Mother. We must go somewhere to show off our newest fashions!" Gracie chimed in.

Lena just froze. She had almost forgotten that three other people in her family even existed.

Charlotte and Grace stopped as Lena bounded into the kitchen. Time stopped. Lois could cut the awkward tension with a knife. She decided it was time to try to dispel these cumbersome occurrences once and for all.

"Uh, girls? Why don't you go upstairs and find a place for your new clothes? I'd like to talk to Lena."

Lena was disappointed. This was the relationship she wanted with her mother, but she was just too different from her sisters. Lorenzo always told Lena that she was just as stubborn as Lois and she knew that was true, although she would never outwardly admit it.

"Hello, Mother. Seems like you had a ... fruitful ... trip."

Lois was obviously nervous. She picked up a dishcloth and anxiously began cleaning a countertop that obviously did not need scrubbing. "I was going to get you some things, Lena ... but ..."

Lena put her hand on the dishcloth so her mother would stop foolishly cleaning. "But you don't really know me, do you, Mother? Why are you here? You hate this ranch."

Lois put the dishcloth in the sink. She turned around and leaned against it. "That why I want to talk to you. And hate is a strong word."

Lena took a defensive stance against the butcher's block in the center of the kitchen. Both women looked as uncomfortable as could be.

"Oh?"

"Yes. Lena, your sisters have no interest in this ranch."

Lena felt very defensive. "That's not true! Allie has grown to love it here!"

Lois had to agree with that. "Okay, yes. I will have to give you the exception of Allison."

There was another painful and awkward silence, so Lena decided to push the issue. "So ..."

Lois motioned for Lena to come over to the table to sit with her. She didn't like the face-off position they were both in. Once they sat down, Lois proceeded.

"Let the twins out of your father's clause. Let them have their inheritance so they can move on with their lives. I'll give you the ranch."

"And Zars and the rest of the horses?"

"All of it. I don't need or want any of it. I just want one thing, Lena."

Lena looked at her mother suspiciously. "Okay. What's that?"

Lois held out her hand. "The chip, Lena."

Lena looked incredibly confused. She let out a nervous laugh and just looked at her mother. "What in the world are you talking about? What chip?"

Lois pulled her hand back and placed it on the table. "That huge chip implanted on your shoulder, Helena. I want you to give the twins and me a chance."

Lena just looked in disbelief at her mother as Eli's words came back to haunt her. Maybe she was being very unfair

She got up and looked out the window for a few minutes and watched Allie and Dirk working Zars with huge smiles on their faces. Dirk kissed Allie on the nose as he hoisted her into the saddle. Hunter walked his horse into a lunge as William explained some things to him. Eli walked Lena's horse out of the stable into the barn. He caught her eye and winked at her.

Everyone was happily playing a part at the ranch. It was Lena who was harboring resentment and not allowing herself to be a part of everyone else's joy. That fact was unfolding right in front of her.

She looked over at her mother, who was just staring at her. Lois felt she needed to continue once Lena faced her.

"I'm sorry, Lena. I'm sorry that I betrayed you. I'm so sorry that life ended up such a mess. Please know that I love you. I know I don't always understand you. But that doesn't mean I don't love you." Lois stood up from the table.

Lena met her halfway and hugged her.

"Mama, I'm sorry things have been so strained between us. I am willing to try. I love you, too. But you'll never get the twins to try with me. They hate me!"

Lena could hear a soft voice speak behind her. "We don't hate you! You are just so stubborn, Helena Joy! And, so strong!" Lena turned around to see Gracie standing there.

Charlie decided to give her two cents. "Yeah! We have no choice but to be stronger. But we would like to try too!"

Gracie and Charlie came from the stairs and flanked Lena on each side. They were so tall and graceful. Lena always felt so small and inferior just standing between them.

"Come out with us tomorrow night. It will be fun! They are supposed to have karaoke at that saloon downtown. We will get Allie and Galen to come! Galen is an awful singer."

Lena looked at them, surprised. "You guys have heard Gale sing?"

Lois looked at her girls. "Lena, that chip on your shoulder has caused you to miss out on a lot. Why don't you go out and enjoy your family for once? Nothing is going to fall in."

Lena looked at her mother, then each sister. "I am a more terrible singer than Galen."

Charlie hugged Lena. *"Awesome!* That makes it more fun, ya know,"

Lena just looked at her, dumbfounded. Then, she giggled. That giggle turned into a sly smile as she looked at her mother. "I'll go on one condition. Mother, you are coming with us!"

Lois looked at them, surprised. "What? That is completely ridiculous. Me? At karaoke? You are ridiculous!"

Lena narrowed her eyes and her mom knew she meant business.

Lois sighed. "Well? I guess I'm going to karaoke with my kids tomorrow."

Gracie clapped her hands together. "Excellent!"

Lois was the sly one this time. "I will be bringing a guest, though."

All three girls' heads turned as if they were snapping right off their necks. In unison, all three said, "Who?"

Lois chuckled. "Ladies. I'm not about to give away my tricks! You shall see."

Lena was both a little bit excited and a little bit uneasy. Lena was sly, but Lois was the queen.

CHAPTER 20

Not sure how to prepare for her first night of karaoke with her family, Lena pulled on a figure-framing navy-blue lace sundress, a pair of cowboy boots, and let her hair down. Finding some makeup in the bathroom, she chose just enough to bring out her features. The finishing touches were the sapphire earrings her father had given her for graduation. Standing back from the mirror, she smiled approvingly. She had to admit that she felt pretty and excited this evening.

"You. Are. Beautiful." Eli was standing in the doorway. Lena blushed. Eli was giving her that "my heart is racing, and I can't speak" look that made her stomach do somersaults.

"Are you sure you won't come with me?" she said, fixing her lipstick one last time.

Eli pushed off the doorjamb with his shoulder and sauntered across the room. For a cowboy, he was so graceful and gentle. There was a soft and supple quality about him that few rarely got to see outside of his rugged exterior.

"Dirk and I were talking about that. This is a family affair, Lena. Besides. Dirk and I are going to head to the lake and fish a little. If we are both dating sisters, we ought to get to know each other."

Lena went over and kissed his cheek. "Such a good plan. I could go for some trout on the grill if you catch some big ones!" Eli saluted her as if meeting the challenge.

Then, Eli kissed Lena tenderly on the cheek. He whispered, "You really do look stunning, Helena."

Lena knew that bedroom voice. "Oh, no, you don't! I'm already late, Eli. You put those bedroom eyes and that sexy voice away!"

Eli chuckled. "You better get out of here, then. I only have so much resistance."

Lena had finished putting her bracelet on at the comment and flew downstairs. Eli hurried down after her and caught her just before she went out the door. He pulled her in for a long, passionate kiss. "Have fun tonight, sweet girl."

Sweet girl was what he always called her. "You stay out of trouble, handsome boy." Handsome boy was her term of endearment. It wasn't too risqué ... but it was theirs. With that, she kissed him again and walked out the door.

The saloon wasn't what Lena expected. It was nice. Clean, cheery, and rustic. Lena found Allie and Gale right away.

Gale was obviously impressed with Lena's appearance. "Well! Look who cleans up like a model! How did Eli let you out of the house like that?"

Lena flushed. "He almost didn't!"

Then, she changed her tune. "Besides, Gale. It's not like I walk around like an ogre all day!"

Galen teased back. "Good thing. No man would ever get anything done if you walked around like that all the time."

Lena decided to tease him back. "Well, maybe I'll start and see what happens."

Galen rolled his eyes. "Great. Just what I wanted to do. Quit my job as a successful lawyer to become a bodyguard."

Allie just smiled, loving their banter, and not believing she had missed it all these years. She was jealous of the bond Lena and Galen had and secretly hoped she could have a bond with them just like it someday.

Just then, Lena heard a giggle she knew all too well. No one knew how to work a room like Charlotte Maleno, with Gracie as the perfect wingman.

"Boys! Really. This is a family evening. You'll have to sing me a song if you want to catch my attention."

All five-ten of Charlotte and Gracie waltzed into the room as if their own theme song were playing. Their perfect figures and tight, yet respectably fitting clothes made an impact. Charlie had on a red dress that showed ample cleavage and even more lavish leg. Allie and Lena just looked at each other. If they put on that dress, it would be at their ankles. A shy little wave, a pop of her foot, and a wave of her hand, and Charlie sashayed out of one room and into the other.

Every man in the bar noticed the entrance of Charlotte and Gracie Maleno.

"Howdy, everyone!" Charlie took a seat and waved at a few men at a table across the room while Gracie blew them a kiss.

"Yes, hello!" Gracie sat down and waved at Allie.

"Hi, ladies." Lena was trying, at least.

"You two sure know how to make an entrance!" Allie had seen it many times before. She was just stating the obvious.

The five siblings were chatting and laughing, not noticing anyone else come in. Finally, they heard a voice. "Well. How are my favorite people this evening?"

Looking up, they saw Lois. Allie rose to greet her with a hug. "Oh! Mother! I didn't see you come in. I'm so sorry."

Lois just laughed. "It's okay. It warms my heart to see all of you jabbering to each other like you were. I must admit, I didn't think I would ever see that."

Lena couldn't tell if that was a snide remark or a proud one.

Galen couldn't take the suspense anymore. "Mother, who is this mystery guest the girls are telling me about?"

"Guests. Plural. And, they just walked in."

Lena swallowed hard as two gentlemen approached. She smiled politely, then turned around and spat at her mother. "Mother. You didn't!"

"The chip, Lena." Lois figuratively held out her hand.

Lena sulked as William and Hunter nervously approached.

Cautiously, William greeted the table. "Hello, all."

Hunter followed. "Yes, hello! I hope this is okay."

The siblings all froze, then looked at each other. Lois rolled her eyes. "This is a family outing. You are family."

Lena felt like the walls were closing in on her.

Allie looked over at Lena, whispering, "Are you okay, Lena?"

"Yes, Allie. I'm okay."

Lena seemed to catch her breath. Once she did, she was able to refocus and engage in conversation. Soon the awkward introductions turned into lighthearted conversations. The night surprisingly passed effortlessly, and Lena found herself laughing and giggling with her siblings.

Many potential suitors sang for Gracie and Charlie, and they ridiculously cheered on each one. Galen pretended to be the big brother and teasingly heckled every man that got on stage to sing for them. The night wore on and patrons at the bar were becoming more social. Hunter eventually joined in with Galen, and the two of them started taunting the potential suitors as the overprotective patriarchs of the Maleno women. The men on stage would react just as humorously, causing the patrons to roar in laughter. Allie and Lena had never laughed so hard.

"Do you guys remember when Gale went through his *Rocky* stage?" Lena asked the table, causing everyone to burst out into laughter, except Galen.

Lois added, "Oh my! He was so cute! He went everywhere shirtless and yelled, 'ADRIAN!'"

Galen pouted. Finally, he muttered, "I hate you people. And that was a good movie, by the way!" That comment only made everyone at the table roar into laughter. "Hey. I was the *only* boy! What did you expect?"

His sisters followed that comment with a very non-sincere, "Aw." "We're sorry, Galen."

Suddenly, everyone at the table stopped teasing Galen, recognizing a familiar voice that was coming from the microphone.

"Good evening, everyone." At the microphone was a very drunk Derek Hopstef, slurring his speech terribly.

Hunter looked horrified, whipping around to obtain a better look at the stage. "Oh no! I'm so sorry! I messed up again. I made the mistake of telling him I was coming here tonight! He wanted to hang out. He promised he was over everything and told me he was going to catch up with an old friend from high school. I thought he was going to do that."

Lena was flabbergasted. "You still talk to him?"

Hunter was very cautious with his response. "Well … yeah …"

All eyes were back on the stage. "I'd like to dedicate this song …"

Derek couldn't really form coherent sentences. It was obvious that the DJ was contemplating whether to allow this to go on or to pull him off stage.

"To my good friends, the Malenos!" Trying to point to the Maleno family, Derek fell back and right onto the stage, hard.

The DJ ran up to him, whispering, although the mic picked up everything. "Yo, dude. Maybe you should have some coffee or something—"

"No!" Derek yelled at the DJ into the mic. "It's my turn! Now play!"

The DJ returned to his computer.

Suddenly, the opening to "Friends in Low Places" by Garth Brooks echoed throughout the saloon.

Galen made the first decision to leave. "I don't think it's a great idea for me to stay here for the ending."

Allie, his ride, nodded and followed him out.

"Galen Maleno, leaving so soon?" Derek was taunting him from the microphone and laughing at his own joke. Allie turned around for a moment, but Galen kept on walking. No one in the bar was laughing or talking.

Hunter looked, distressed, at everyone at the table. "I'm so sorry, everyone. When he comes off stage, I'll gather him up and take him home."

The song continued, and Derek began to sing, slurring words together and staggering all over the stage.

Lena stood up and grabbed her purse. "In the meantime, I'm out as well. Good night, everyone."

Lois decided she better leave, too. "I'll walk out with you, Lena."

"And you can kiss my ..." Derek, believing everyone would join in the lyrics, stopped. A few bars later, the DJ kindly stopped the music. Not knowing what to do next, everyone in the bar froze.

Lena pushed her chair in. "Yep! Time to go. See you guys later."

The sound of Lena's boots on the dance floor broke the awkward silence. Lois, seeing a streak of blond out of the corner of her right eye, stopped, and shrieked, but it was too late. Derek leaped off stage toward Lena, pulling her purse off her shoulder while the contents scattered all over the dance floor. Lena was aghast at the situation.

"Lena! Don't go. I love you! Stay here. Go home with me!" Derek had ahold of her hand this time, pulling it toward him.

The bouncer immediately lunged for Derek, putting himself between the two of them. Lois turned Lena and pushed her out the side exit. She and Lois continued to their cars. Hunter and William helped the bouncer pick Derek up from the floor while Gracie and Charlie picked up Lena's belongings.

"He can't come back here," the bouncer said to Hunter.

"I've got it. He won't be returning on my watch, sir."

Derek suddenly passed out in Hunter and William's arms, prompting the owner of the bar to join the bouncer. "I don't think he should make a repeat appearance here." The owner gave a serious look to William and Hunter.

"I think this man and I will be parting ways after this, sir," Hunter said. "If he returns, it will not be because of me, I assure you."

The owner nodded as Hunter and William carried Derek out the door and loaded him into their truck.

CHAPTER *21*

Lena was brushing Zars the next morning, which was unusual. Zars was an athlete on a schedule. Lena knew that interrupting his routine even for just a bit was a bad idea.

"What are you doing?" Dirk was confused. Lena didn't often concern herself with Zars. She usually brushed Myrna every morning, then started her trail-riding schedule for the day.

Lena was annoyed by Dirk's remark, although she knew she shouldn't be. She just wanted to brush and admire Zars. However, she knew she was throwing Dirk off by pulling Zars out on her own and throwing off his routine.

"He's my horse, Dirk." The way Lena was talking was curt and short, which confused Dirk. He knew to tread lightly. Lena was either having a bad day or there was something very seriously wrong.

Finally, Allie came upon the situation. "Lena, what's going on here?"

Dirk looked relieved.

"Can't I just brush a thoroughbred when I feel like it?" Lena snapped again.

Allie felt the same as Dirk, suddenly. She looked worriedly at Dirk, trying to read his face for some clue. Allie decided she better tread lightly as well. "Of course. But, Zars is on a strict schedule and you know that. Seems something is going on with you."

Very sarcastically, Lena responded. "Well! I wouldn't want to mess with Zars' schedule, now, would I?"

Lena seemed very cool and calculated while Allie and Dirk remained wary. Lena was unsure of why she felt out of sorts. Of course, Allie and Dirk were right for bringing all of this up with her. She was the one in the wrong for acting like she was, but she was struggling with anxiety.

Lena decided to walk up to the barn, hoping the anxiety would dissipate by the time she arrived.

Eli was in a pair of tight-fitting Wrangler jeans and a black tank top. His tan muscles were bulging out everywhere and he wore a smile on his face under his Pirates baseball cap. "Hey, sweet girl." Before Lena knew it, he pulled her into his arms. His scent was intoxicating. She leaned her head into his chest and just allowed herself to be pulled into the safety of his arms.

Eli kissed her on the top of the head. "I missed you. Hunter told me what happened last night. I'm so sorry, baby. Are you okay?"

Lena just frowned. "I don't know. I thought I was. I guess Derek really has me rattled. You know how much I hate being embarrassed in public places."

Eli pulled her away from his chest and looked at her sympathetically. "I have no doubt. I would be rattled. How about a ride to the fence before your trail ride?"

Lena looked a little more relieved. "Yes. That would clear my head a bit. And I want to check on that fence. William said it was finished yesterday. That will determine the course of my trail ride today."

Lena and Eli saddled their horses and were off.

Lena was correct. She could feel her head clear and her anxiety start to leave her body as she trotted out into the field.

Eli looked over at her mischievously. "Lena?"

Lena was just breathing in the fresh air with her eyes closed. "Yes, Eli?"

"Catch me if ya can!" Then he took off.

Lena's eyes snapped open. "No fair!" She kicked Myrna, whistled, and yelled, "Come on, girl. We can't let this happen!"

Lena took off, knowing she would never catch Eli. He was a great rider. She loved feeling the wind in her hair. It felt like she was flying. Eli made it to the fence and instantly turned his horse around.

Suddenly, Lena saw a flash of blinding light. She let go of her right rein and shielded her eyes as Myrna reared up. At the speed she was going, she couldn't hold on. She was thrown from Myrna as Myrna ran for the barn.

"LENA!" Lena could hear Eli's scream as she hit the ground with a thud. Lena's world went black.

Eli raced for Lena, dismounting Lakota before he even stopped. Eli lifted her head in his hands and held her close. "Oh no. No, no no no no no!"

He felt his chest tighten and his eyes fill with tears.

Eli cradled her head and rocked back and forth repeatedly, stroking her hair, and begging her to come back to him. He noticed blood, but he couldn't tell where it was coming from.

Back at the barn, Allie and Dirk saw Myrna come in, sans Lena. They knew something was wrong. Allie instantly mounted Zars and followed the path Myrna had just taken.

Dirk yelled after Allie, "Whoa, Zars!"

Zars halted. "Where do you think you're going?"

"I'm going to see what happened! Lena would never be without Myrna!"

Dirk called for Hunter and explained what happened. He pulled Remington, his paint horse, out of the barn. Dirk pulled himself onto Remington without a saddle and kicked him toward the hayfield. Hunter stood there, awestruck. No cowboy he knew could successfully ride a horse bareback at any speed, and certainly not a horse as large as Remington.

Dirk and Allie got to the fence in record time. Eli was taking Lena's pulse and was trying to get her to drink water. He was pouring it over her lips, hoping it would enter her mouth.

Allie hopped off Zars. Magnificent and intimidating, Zars didn't move an inch. There was no question that tiny little Ali commanded the noble steed and he obeyed. "Eli ... what?"

Eli looked up at them with the most heartbroken eyes they had ever seen. They were filled with tears that started to spill as soon as he looked up, pleading with them. In a voice that was husky and barely audible, Eli looked at Allie. "Help me, please. She's got a strong pulse." Then, he pulled Lena's tiny wrist up to his temple and caressed her hand against his head.

Dirk and Allie were heartbroken for him, but they both snapped into action. Allie went down to Lena's legs and put them on her knees as she hunkered on the ground. It was then that she noticed the blood. Pulling her hand up and looking at it, she gasped as blood dripped from it.

Dirk went over to her instantly. "Allie!"

"It's not mine! It's not mine!" Allie kept looking at Dirk while she was in shock. "It's Lena's! And I can't tell where it's coming from!"

At that moment, they heard a small moan. Lena had come out of her fainting spell a little but was disoriented and weak. She opened her eyes lazily and looked at Eli. She raised her blood-soaked hand just enough to put it on Eli's cheek, causing it to be stained with blood as well. When Lena looked at it, her eyes got big. She looked down at her hand and began to fuss in Eli's arms.

"The ambulance is on its way, but we'll have to get her to the barn, at least. They can't make it up here." Dirk's information seemed to calm everyone a bit.

Eli mounted his horse and Dirk handed Lena to him. He cradled Lena in his arms. Allie and Zars led the way. Before heading down, something caught Dirk's eye. "Will you be okay? I'll be down in a bit."

Allie looked at him suspiciously. "I promise. I'm all good. You've got this, baby."

Allie nodded. Eli and Lena followed. Zars and Lakota slowly walked down the path, carrying their precious cargo.

Dirk watched them for a few seconds to make sure they were going to be okay. Then he dismounted and hopped over the fence, bending down to get a fresh look. He smoothed his hand over fresh horse tracks. One of the tracks suggested that the horse had a bar shoe. None of their horses had been injured recently. Eli shoed every horse on Maleno Ranch. Dirk knew of no horse here that wore a bar shoe or had a hoof injury.

Dirk walked around the tracks … three normal shoes, one bar. Three normal shoes, one bar. The trail led him to another clue.

In a tree was a red ball cap that Dirk recognized. Dirk ran his thumb over a tuft of blond hair that was trapped in the adjuster. On the front of the hat was the Maleno Ranch logo. Dirk made a fist and punched the inside of the hat, knowing exactly who was responsible for this.

Dirk now searched for a clue that told him what Derek had done to spook either Lena or Myrna. Simply seeing Derek was not cause for Lena to fall or for Myrna to rear. Dirk looked for another two hours without finding a single clue. He finally gave up, mounted Remington, and left for the barn.

At the hospital, Eli paced as Allie bit her nails. Her mother always scolded her since she was eight years old about biting her nails. They both looked up with hopeful eyes as a short, stout woman entered the waiting room.

"Hi. I'm Dr. Pizano. Is there a family member here?"

Allie spoke up. "I'm her sister, and this is her ... fiancé."

Eli looked at Allie with big eyes. Allie looked back at him with a knowing smile. Eli smiled back.

Dr. Pizano nodded. "The good news? It will take a little while, but Helena will eventually be fine. I have every confidence that she will make a full recovery. She took a very nasty fall, as you know, and she needs a lot of rest."

Eli let out a very long, relieved breath. Then, he looked questioningly at Dr. Pizano. "Wait. You said that's good news. Is there bad news? Because that sounds like perfect news."

Dr. Pizano put her hand on Eli's shoulder. Eli started to panic. "I'm so sorry, Mr. ..."

"Miller. My name is Eli Miller."

"Miller. I'm so sorry, Mr. Miller. We were not able to save the baby. The fall caused Helena to miscarry."

Eli's face fell and he turned pale white. Allie and Dr. Pizano led him to a chair and sat him down.

"Is there anything I can do?"

"No," Allie said. "Thank you, Dr. Pizano. That will be all."

Eli just looked at Allie in shock. Allie instinctively pulled him in for a hug as her eyes filled with tears. Eli was unable to produce an emotion. He was suddenly in a trance.

CHAPTER 22

Eli pulled away from Allie in disbelief.

"Eli, are you okay?" Allie started chewing her fingernails again, this time adding the nervous tapping of her foot. She was uncomfortable in crisis situations. When times were tough, she usually let Galen handle things. Comforting Eli was out of the box for her.

Eli silently got up and slowly walked to the window, looking outside for a few seconds. He started talking to whoever would listen. "She has no idea."

Allie tilted her head. "Eli. Are you sure? How do you know?"

Eli just kept talking to the window. "She said earlier that she felt out of sorts. She thought it was just because of Derek. She didn't know it was hormonal. I raced her to the fence. I should have known ..."

Allie got up and went to Eli. "Eli. You can't blame yourself."

Eli finally looked at her, harshly spewing the words of his guilt. "Then who am I to blame?"

Allie just looked at him with sympathy. "No one. This was an accident. It was no one's fault."

Eli just turned his head back to the scene beyond the window.

The doctor came in and interrupted them again.

"Mr. Miller? Ms. Maleno is asking for you. I said just a few minutes was all she was allowed. There is more news."

Eli turned from the window. He looked at her. "More news?"

"Yes. Before, we were able to stop the hemorrhage in her abdomen."

Eli was getting annoyed with the step-by-step approach. "And now?"

Dr. Pizano was wringing her hands nervously. "There seems to be a clotting issue."

Eli placed his hands on Dr. Pizano's bicep. He couldn't take it anymore. He tried not to sound aggressive but was unsuccessful. "Will you please just be direct, Dr. Pizano?" Every word he spoke was more biting than the previous one.

Allie got between them and gently pulled Eli's hands from Dr. Pizano. "Eli. How about we all come and sit over here?"

Eli began nervously raking his fingers through his hair as they all sat in a corner. "Dr. Pizano. Can you please tell us what that means?"

Dr. Pizano let out a deep breath and sighed. "If we go in surgically, I can't be certain she won't have an emergency hysterectomy. The fall has caused some very nasty internal bleeding. We are trying our best."

Eli put his head in his hands, so Allie instinctively put her hand on his back. "Eli? She needs to know if she can do surgery. I'll sign, but I need to know what you want to do."

Eli picked up his head. He was working at it, but his words were calmer. "Yes, of course. You must save her. God will do the rest." He closed his eyes as if repeating a small prayer to himself.

Eli left Allie to the paperwork and walked somberly toward Lena's hospital room. Lena, the tower of strength, was so weak and small. He just wanted to scoop her up and take her home, where he could hold her forever.

He ran to her side and sat down, holding her hand. "Hi, sweetie."

A very weak Lena turned her head and managed a small smile. She croaked out a "hi."

Eli put his hand on her forehead and pushed her hair back. "How are you feeling?"

Lena suddenly had fire in her eyes. "Stupid. Eli? What's going on? Do these people think I've lost my brain?"

Eli just looked down. Suddenly, something arose in him. He didn't know why, but he started laughing. Lena began to get furious. Eli tried to stop laughing.

"What is so funny?"

Eli just kissed her hand. "You almost died in my arms. I think the world is ending, and the first thing you ask is if people think you've lost your brain. Oh, Lena, how I love you."

Lena was suddenly as furious as she could be for as weak as she was. "Eli Miller. You must tell me the truth! You are the one person in this world I depend on!" The content of her words was fierce and exactly what she would say. Listening to her made Eli evaporate into a pool of sadness. Her voice was hoarse and had no strength behind it. Lena was no longer invincible, and he had taken her for granted.

Eli put his head down and began to cry. Lena suddenly put her hand on the back of his head. "Oh, Eli! I'm so sorry."

Eli just kept crying. All of these mixed-up emotions just kept flooding out of him. "Lena. I just can't …" He looked up to find a horrified look on Lena's face.

Eli stood up and looked out another window as he searched for words. He had no idea how to break this kind of news to

the woman he loved more than anything in the world. Eli put
his hands on the sides of the window and bowed his head as
Lena looked at him with heartbreak and fear. She tried to give
him time to work through whatever he was trying to say, but the
longer it took for him to process it, the more terrified she became.

"Don't make him tell you, child." They both looked at the
door to see Lois standing there.

"Mother!"

Lois put her hand on Eli's shoulder ever so delicately.
Her voice was soft and matronly. Lena remembered that voice
when Daddy died. "Eli. Why don't you get something from the
cafeteria? I need a few minutes alone with my daughter."

Eli looked at Lena and kissed her hand again. Lena nodded
and patted his hand. "It's okay, baby. She's right. I know you
haven't eaten, and I'm okay. Please go." Maybe this was all too
much for Eli, so soon after the death of his mother. She was
worried about him.

Eli hugged Lois and sweetly kissed Lena on the lips.
"Helena Maleno, please don't ever forget how much I love you.
Please."

Lena's heart melted. She must have scared him so. "I love
you too, Eli Miller."

Eli exited with tears in his eyes.

Lois took Eli's seat. "Allie told me what happened."

Lois suddenly looked very matter-of-fact in her expression
and Lena didn't know what to make of it.

"So, you'll tell me? And you'll be perfectly honest?"

"Aren't I always?"

Lena smiled. Besides this thing with William, her mother
had always been brutally honest with her. It was one of her best
qualities.

"This all happened to Eli, too, my sweet. Don't torture him by making him say the words just yet."

Lena looked thoroughly confused. "What words?"

Lois took Lena's hand this time. "You lost a child, Helena. Eli's child."

Lena just looked at her mother as if she were unable to comprehend what she said. Lois was quick to realize what Lena was thinking. "Lena, you heard me correctly. You were pregnant, you just didn't realize it yet. The fall from Myrna caused you to miscarry."

Lena thought she should cry, but the tears did not come. This was an emotion Lena was unable to fathom or comprehend. Lois was talking, but nothing was registering in her mind. There were words swirling around in her head. Baby. Eli. Pregnant. Miscarriage. Those words were all clashing against each other, and none of them made sense. None of them landed in the correct order to make a legitimate sentence.

Lena's expression suddenly went far away. Expecting this, Lois could tell that she was gone to a place inside of herself. Lena was better than all her children at putting up walls. And she was the best at fortifying them, too.

Lois suddenly went on defense. "Now, Lena. Allie, Eli, and Dirk all say that fall was not your fault."

Lois was rambling again as Lena began to replay everything in her mind. She was doing odd things, outside of her normal routine. Eli had raced her to the fence. She should have been able to handle that. Myrna should have, too. Why did this ...

Lena suddenly looked at her mother as if she were in a trance. "The flash of light ..."

Lois stopped and looked at Lena, not hearing her at first. "What did you say, dear?" There was no repetition. She was in a trance, and Lois was unable to find her. She was lost in her own mind and was not processing anything now. Lena was reliving it all in her mind. Lois was a bystander as Lena replayed it all in her head. She knew the moment Lena fell as the tears came tumbling down her cheeks. Her voice became ragged and hoarse.

When Lois realized she was finished reliving the event in her mind, Lena turned and asked for Eli in a barely audible whisper. She was just staring straight forward. Lois was frightened for her.

"Mama. Can Eli come back, please?"

Lois became panicked. "I will go find him right now."

She turned her head slightly. "Mother?"

Lois stopped dead in her tracks. "Yes, Helena?"

Lena could barely get the words out before she burst into tears.

"Thank you, Mama. I love you." Lena had realized what happened. Now was the moment the insurmountable emotional pain took over.

Lois' heart broke into a million pieces. She had never felt pain like this in her whole life. Not even when Lorenzo died. She could only imagine what Lena felt and imagining it hurt like hell.

When Eli came in, he crawled into bed with Lena. He held her close and just cried with her. No one made mention of Lena's continuing medical danger. Right now, it was just mourning the loss of the child of whom they were unaware but loved with all their hearts.

CHAPTER 23

Eli tried to visit Lena the following morning, but she was already in surgery. The doctor asked him to go back to the ranch and bring her some of her favorite, comfortable clothes for recovery. Although Eli didn't want to leave, he felt that pacing in the waiting room was going to drive him mad. Most of the family was at the hospital and just kept apologizing and looking at him with eyes of sympathy, which only made him feel worse. He took the doctor's suggestion and went to the ranch to get Lena some clothes. Not wanting him to be alone, Allie tagged along, which he found both annoying and endearing.

The drive to the ranch was filled with awkward silence. Socializing was the last thing on Eli's mind, and Allie was awkward in these situations. He was grateful as he turned into the lane that led to the ranch house, until he saw something that unnerved him. Hunter was going into the barn with a shotgun.

Eli barreled out of the truck with Allie, who was much faster when running for the barn. They got there just as Hunter was tying Myrna to a post, then took aim.

"Hunter!" Allie's scream seemed to reverberate throughout the entire barn, stopping everything.

Hunter slowly lowered his gun and Myrna whinnied. Eli stopped as he entered the gate while Hunter slowly turned around, catching his breath.

"What are you doing, Hunter?" A furious Eli walked over and took the gun out of Hunter's hand.

Hunter looked at Eli pleadingly. "Eli. You need to go. You need to get out of here."

Allie looked panicked. "What do you think you're doing?"

Hunter put his hand on her shoulder. "Allie, Dirk said he just couldn't do it, so William took him out of here. I said I would, and I'd bury her, too."

He walked over to Eli. "Eli, she's lame. You know she's suffering. You know she's in so much pain. More than we know."

"She wasn't lame when she came back down from the field! I know she wasn't!"

Hunter looked away.

Allie went over and forcefully turned Hunter toward him. Her tiny finger started pointing into his chest. "You better tell me what's going on right now!" Although Allie wasn't the slightest bit intimidating, Hunter grabbed her finger, put it down to her side, and began his explanation.

"Dirk thought he would lunge Myrna today instead of Zars. Try to settle her down some."

"And?" Allie was growing impatient.

Hunter slowly walked away from them. "There was a trap. It was set way in the mud, out of anyone's eyesight. It was meant for Zars. Myrna took it instead."

Eli flushed pale and had to sit down. Allie flushed the same color of white, so she sat as well. "Oh … my …." Allie didn't finish her sentence.

Hunter sat down between them. "You could have been on Zars when he stepped in that trap, Allie."

Eli tried to control his anger. He stood up and started to pace. Allie and Hunter watched him cautiously for a few seconds. "Why was there a trap in the middle of my round pen?" Eli uncharacteristically yelled.

Hunter looked down for a moment, causing Eli to walk over and stand right in front of him. "Hunter, you look at me ..."

Hunter looked up, conflicted about whether to tell Eli the truth, given the state of mind he was in.

"For the same reason Dirk found hoofprints up at the fence where Lena fell. One of the hoofprints was strange ... not from any of our horses."

For the first time ever, Allie thought she could see flames in Eli's eyes. She didn't know that Eli had fire deep within his soul. "That all?"

Hunter began to stutter.

Eli grabbed him by the shirt collar and pulled him off the bale in one swooping motion. "I said. Is. That. All!"

Allie got between the two of them before Eli got any more heated. "Eli. Put him down. Please."

Eli looked down at his hand and dropped Hunter as if he suddenly came to his senses. He just looked at his hand in disbelief, as if it had a mind of its own when it had jerked Hunter from the bale.

"Hunter ... I'm so sorry ... I don't ..."

Hunter didn't allow him to finish. "No apologizing. I can't imagine what I would do if I'd been through even half of what you've been through. Please. I don't accept apologies that aren't necessary."

Eli nodded graciously, putting distance between him and Hunter. "Please. Tell me the rest." Eli made sure he was calmer, quieter, and more in control.

Hunter felt better about telling Eli the rest. It was like he had come to his senses.

"Dirk also found a Maleno cap with a few blond hairs in the adjuster."

Eli just kept stroking Myrna and looking at her broken leg. Suddenly something dawned on him as he looked up at Hunter. "Was it red?"

Hunter just nodded suspiciously. "How did you know that?"

Eli stopped touching Myrna and grabbed his hat that had fallen to the ground as he started for the gate.

"Wait! Where are you going?" Allie asked in desperation.

"Dirk, William, and Galen are already on the search," Hunter blurted out.

Eli stopped and lowered his head. He turned around and looked at Hunter, exasperated. "What am I supposed to do?"

Hunter turned to Eli sympathetically. "You go in that house and get Lois. Then, you, Lois, and Allie take Lena some comfortable clothes. You make sure you're gone for a long while. I have a lot to do here this evening."

"I don't think anyone should be alone here, Hunter."

Hunter added, "I won't be. My brother is on his way. He's going to help me bury Myrna and ..."

Eli looked at him curiously. "And what?"

Hunter didn't want to tell everyone his news like this. It seemed too odd. "Well? He's a jockey. He's going to jockey for me."

Eli thought for a few seconds. "I don't think anyone should take any horses out right now."

Hunter nodded in agreement. "I agree. Right now, I think it would be wise to comb the ranch for anymore hidden surprises. I think once we take care of Myrna and the guys get back, we will set out to do so."

Allie chimed in. "I like that idea!"

Hunter gently pushed both toward the gate. "Can you be gone in about fifteen minutes? The vet was here. He said Myrna is not only lame but in insurmountable pain. She's been such a sweet horse. I don't want her to suffer anymore."

Allie looked at him sadly. "I'll go get Mother now."

Before she left, Allie went over and kissed Myrna on the nose. "Bye, Myrna. We love you."

Eli thought it just couldn't get any worse. Then he remembered. He had to tell Lena.

CHAPTER 24

Lena woke up the next morning feeling raw and totally exposed. Everything was an irritation for her. The slightest sound was heightened. The light from the hall seemed to glare and hurt her eyes. The buzz of the hospital was unnerving. The sedative had worn off at 4:13 a.m. according to the clock in her room. The silence was the most deafening sound of all.

Lena looked straight ahead. She tried to feel something. Anything. But there was nothing to feel. She just felt ... blank. She had known nothing of her pregnancy. Her opportunity to enjoy that was now taken away and she could only hope God would bless her again, but no one knew if that would be the case. The anxiety she felt that wretched day had never registered in her mind as a baby. Her chance to enjoy being a mother was gone. What stung the most was that her child had not been taken by nature. Blaming God or fate would do her no good. In Lena's mind, this was no accident, this was murder, and someone should have to pay for that.

She'd had no time to bond with her baby and now she was here, undeservedly. The world she knew was far away, and she now lived on another planet with a population of one. Everyone that asked how she was feeling irritated her, and everyone that tried to be nice irritated her even more. She tried to smile and pretend she was fine, but that made her a liar. Her body hurt, and her soul was crushed. There was no part of her that could possibly endure the torture that was feeding from her mind. There was no sleep as nightmares only replayed in her imagination. The occasional happy dream starred her, Eli, and baby, living happily ever after. She was unsure which was the lesser of two evils.

Lena decided she wanted to sit in the recliner beside her bed and look out the window to evade sleep. But when she tried to get up, all hell broke loose. Bells started to go off and lights started to flash. It was at this moment that Lena realized she was wearing some sort of diaper and she was in the intensive care unit.

Lena's heart jumped and she immediately started to panic. "What did I do? What's going on?" She grabbed a nurse and asked the same thing, only this time she looked the nurse square in the eye and asked the same questions with venom. The nurse seemed afraid, convincing Lena that something was very wrong.

The nurse looked back at her. "I ... can go get a doctor for you. You aren't allowed out of bed, Ms. Maleno. Is there anything I can get you?"

The beautiful nurse had the most gorgeous complexion Lena had ever seen. Her skin was the color of cinnamon. Her hair was comprised of small ringlets that were pulled into a ponytail that reached the middle of her back. Some of the ringlets escaped the ponytail and framed her face. She had super-long eyelashes that most people mistakenly thought were fake. She was a striking woman. Of course, she was as tall as Charlie and Gracie, which made Lena jealous.

"Answers! I want answers ... Rebecca!" She looked down long enough to see the nurse's name tag. "Rebecca Smiley? *Seriously?*"

The nurse snatched her name tag out of Lena's grasp. "Yes. *Nurse* Smiley is my name. Now, can I help you, Ms. Maleno?"

Nurse Smiley's tone suggested she was a contender for Lena's fiery personality. Lena would not step on her toes!

Lena started to bark orders. She felt like absolute hell, and people were eluding her. Things were going to get ugly.

"Either someone tells me what's up, or I will sign myself out of here!"

Rebecca tried to calm Lena down. "Okay. Ms. Maleno, please be still. I'm really not supposed to tell you what your diagnosis is! But we had a major crash come in. I know it will be a while until a doctor comes, and leaving would be detrimental to you right now."

Lena fearfully glanced up at Rebecca, who had successfully caught her attention. "Detrimental? Why?"

Rebecca sighed and took a seat in the recliner that Lena had been aiming for. "Please know that I'm not a doctor. In fact, I've really not been a nurse for very long! Just two years …"

Lena was growing impatient. "Rebecca, get on with it."

Rebecca swallowed hard and grabbed her chart. "Okay. There was a lot of internal bleeding when you fell. They thought they had it under control when you first came in. But you started bleeding again soon after. They were hoping it was just trauma from the miscarriage, even though you had the necessary procedure."

Lena just looked away. Yeah, the necessary procedure for a miscarriage, she meant.

"When you were still bleeding after that, they did some exploratory surgery. They really wanted to rule out a hysterectomy, seeing that you are so young."

Lena could feel her already fragile nerves crash. She had to find the strength to battle this to find out what happened to her child. If someone had caused this and she was never going to be able to carry another child, someone was going to pay!

"What did they find?"

Rebecca smiled at her. "They found a laceration in your liver. When they went in for the surgery, they repaired it. You *must* lie here and allow it to heal properly. You will get blood drawn, which might seem excessive, but you have to promise me to behave."

Rebecca smiled sweetly and seemed to put Lena at ease.

"And the ... hysterectomy?" Lena added.

Rebecca smiled and touched her arm. "What hysterectomy? Not for you, Ms. Maleno. Who knows? Maybe you'll have twins one day!" Lena sighed with relief.

Rebecca chided her again. "Now, behave. I mean it. You must stay in this bed!"

Lena gave her a half smile. "Thank you, Rebecca, for being honest with me and not treating me like I'm going to break." At the end of her sentence, Lena began to break down. Finally, the tears came, and Lena was ready to allow them.

Rebecca grabbed her hand. "Aw, Lena. Everyone here heard your story, honey. I can't imagine what you are going through. I also couldn't imagine being left in the dark, either." She hugged Lena. Lena seemed to appreciate the gesture. "If you need anything, just buzz."

"Thank you. I think I just need to be alone. Eli will be in soon."

Rebecca gave her another smile. "Sure enough."

For the first time, Lena allowed herself to truly mourn her loss. She mourned the loss of her child while she prayed. She prayed that God would bless her and Eli with another child again, and she asked God to forgive her for every awful thought she ever had. Finally, she thanked God for bringing everyone that loved her to her side. Mostly, she thanked God for Eli. Then she drifted off to sleep.

CHAPTER *25*

The next few days were a blur. It seemed like everything made Lena cry. Once she allowed those floodgates to open, the waterworks never stopped. She no longer turned the TV on. She refused visitors and turned down offers to take therapeutic walks around the hospital. Eli looked so broken and tired when he visited.

He tried to put on a brave face, but Lena knew this was so much more than he could bear. He seemed to be holding so much inside and she knew he didn't want to burden her.

Lena convinced Eli to skip his early morning chores and go into town. She could walk and had been moved out of ICU. There was still a laceration on her liver and one of her kidneys was supposed to function better. However, her numbers looked better each day and the doctor said if they continued to get better over the weekend, she could go home Sunday night.

Lena asked Eli for a decent robe and walking slippers. She was getting stir-crazy and the slipper socks the hospital gave her were uncomfortable.

Lois brought her pajamas and novels. When Lena asked for her laptop, Lois refused and brought her a tablet instead. Lois did not want her working on her laptop.

Lena hated not being able to make her own decisions, yet she was grateful someone else was making her decisions at the same time. It was like there were two different Helena Malenos at war inside of her.

"Hidey ho, little sister! Have no fear!" Gracie came bumbling through the door.

Charlie came next and made a graceful pose. "We have arrived."

Allie was behind them, looking like a pack mule, full of what seemed like tiny luggage. "Yes, they have arrived. I get to carry everything!"

Lena couldn't help but smile. Much to her dismay, the ridiculous nature of her three sisters was what she looked forward to every day.

"What's all this?" Lena asked.

Charlie and Gracie got to work right away, unpacking things all over her room. They had total disregard for the fact that they were in a hospital.

Gracie looked at Lena, dumbfounded. "Lena! This is your makeover!" She rolled her eyes as if Lena should have known this all along.

Charlie acted like this was something everyone on the planet wanted. "What lifts your spirit more than a makeover?"

Lena was awed. "In a hospital? Why do I need a makeover for a hospital?"

Gracie sighed teasingly. "To be the envy of everyone on this floor, of course!"

Charlie began to turn bottles of liquid over as if to mix them up. "Honestly, Lena, how did you survive without us all this time?" Lena wondered if that was a serious question or hypothetical.

Lena and Allie both smiled at each other. The newfound relationship between all the sisters was pleasant. Eli was right. There was a side to her twin sisters that she was growing to love.

Gracie held up a pair of red silk pajamas, which made Charlie turn up her nose.

"Gracie. You can't be serious. Red pajamas on a redhead? Oh. I just can't allow that to happen."

Allie looked horrified. "Hey! My favorite sweatshirt is red!"

Charlie and Gracie just froze at that comment, both desperately searching for something to say.

"Well. This is not your makeover, Allie. We will save you for another day." Gracie said the comment as if it were small talk, but Allie was not amused.

Lena just smiled. There was a time not long ago when Allie would have gone inside herself at that comment instead of rolling her eyes. Lena still hoped Allie would stand up to Charlie and Gracie, but standing her ground was progress. Dirk and Zars had given her a newfound confidence.

The makeover went longer than could be expected because the four women were laughing and joking as Eli walked in.

He stopped in his tracks. His eyes seemed to soften, and his smile broadened across his face as his cheeks got insanely red. It was obvious that he was thinking of Lena in a very erotic way.

"Now *that* … is the reaction I was waiting for. Thanks, Eli!" Eli looked away from Gracie after her comment.

"Our work here is done." Eli didn't often look at Charlie when she said anything.

"I'm not carrying everything back to the car!" Eli chuckled.

The three sisters kissed Lena and talked all at the same time while leaving.

Eli walked slowly to the bed and kissed Lena sweetly. "Oh my. You are so insanely beautiful."

"Oh, Eli." Then Lena began crying, then laughing, causing Eli to look at her suspiciously.

"What's wrong? Or funny?"

Lena just chuckled. "My makeup is running. This is exactly why you don't have makeovers in hospitals!"

Eli just chuckled, kissed her smeared face, and held her close. He knew it would be a long road, but he knew the love of his life was beginning to heal. And so was he.

Chapter 26

Eli was just leaving to get a bite to eat when he came across William and Hunter coming into the small waiting room. He narrowed his eyes suspiciously at the two men.

"Hi." Eli couldn't bring himself to be cordial.

"Hi, Eli!" William sounded cheerful, which just annoyed Eli even more. Emotionally, Lena was finally moving into a better place, not appearing so far away. She was coming back to him. But wherever William was, a tornado followed, and Eli knew he lacked the strength to weather whatever storm William brought his way.

Eli could tell that there was an ulterior motive for this visit. He knew what it was, and he was instantly defensive. Galen filed in soon behind them. Surprised, he narrowed his eyes in suspicion. Eli felt a lot better once Galen showed up, feeling like the calvary had shown for battle.

"Looks like I'm late to the party!" Galen was in a sarcastic mood and seemed just as suspicious of the presence of William and Hunter. Galen's defenses were evident, which meant he and Eli were telepathically on the same page.

William motioned for them all to go down the hall to the cafeteria, where he suggested the men of the family have a talk. Eli and Galen looked at each other. Galen crossed his arms and planted his feet firmly.

"Why?"

William whispered, "You know that once she hears Eli's voice, she's going to want him to come in, so keep your voice down, Gale. I want to discuss something with you."

Galen rolled his eyes and followed. Eli sighed and filed out behind Galen.

Everyone bought a sandwich and a drink and sat down. Eli and Hunter began to speak at the same time, then stopped. Hunter motioned for Eli to continue.

"I know why you're here. You are not telling her about Myrna! She's finally making headway, so you two can just eat your sandwiches and head back to the ranch."

Galen pushed his chair away from the table and put his hands up. "Whoa. Guys. Is that your intention? Are you insane? You can't tell her about Myrna. I knew you two were idiots, but I didn't think you were the biggest idiots on the planet!"

Hunter looked at Galen, insulted. "Gee, thanks, Galen. No, we are not the biggest idiots on the planet. And we *are* thinking about Lena. In fact, we are thinking only of her!"

Eli and Galen just looked at each other in frustration. "You're thinking of Lena? Really. Tell me how this news is thinking about Lena?"

Hunter stopped and put his hands on the table. He took a moment to collect his thoughts. When he spoke again, he made sure his voice was very calm and low. "I don't want to hurt Lena anymore. I really don't. But what do you think is going to happen when she returns to the ranch? Are you just going to tell her Myrna ran away? Are you going to tell her that Myrna is up in the pasture, over and over?"

Eli and Galen both looked at Hunter, then at each other. Neither of them was ready to face that before this moment.

Galen, always a man with answers, had a plan. "Well? We will tell her when she gets there." Eli had been hoping that Galen had a much better plan than that.

It was William who cautiously answered. "Do you think that's wise? Right now, she's near doctors who can help her deal with this one more tragedy. If she has a setback at home, what's your plan?"

Galen and Eli just looked at each other. There was no plan. Eli was in survival mode and was only thinking minute to minute. Galen, who usually bragged about these kinds of things as if they were his claim to fame, had missed this one and was ashamed of himself. Galen, the guy who always had a plan, had to admit defeat this time.

Hunter looked at them with sorrow. "Guys, we have to rip off the Band-Aid. No unexpected surprises for her return home. She's trying to gain strength to return to her life. Let's not throw this at her when she's not expecting it and when she's looking forward to healing."

Eli and Galen looked at each other again. They both knew Hunter was right, no matter how painful the situation was. Eli had a hard time grasping it and he knew he lacked the strength to tell Lena.

Galen was the first to break the silence. "I would like to tell her."

Eli tried to interject, knowing it was the thing to do, but Galen just put up his hand. "Eli, you have gone through so much yourself lately. You need to do some healing yourself. Hunter, you took care of this situation with Myrna when no one else could. William, I know you well enough to know that this isn't your cup of tea. I also know that you would agree that you aren't the best person for this particular job right now, given the circumstances, yes?"

William nodded.

Although grateful, Eli hated that he was allowing Galen to do something that he felt it was his responsibility. He hated that he was in this vulnerable place and that Galen had to take over. "Fine, but I'm there when you tell her!"

"Same."

"Here, too."

Galen was touched by the support all the men showed, but he was also grateful. Although he was being noble, he really didn't want to do this alone. It absolutely killed him to see Lena go through this. He would do absolutely anything to take this pain from her.

"Well? Let's get this over with, then."

The men rode the elevator from the cafeteria to Lena's room in silence. They couldn't even look at each other. When the doors opened, each man sighed to himself, then they walked out, one by one, and strode down the hallway. One nurse began to smile at them, but quickly changed her mind when she saw the look on their faces, thinking maybe they were all going to visit a dying patient.

When they entered the room, they all pasted on ridiculous, fake smiles and tried their best to pretend they were jubilant. Lena was suspicious instantly.

"Well! Look at this. All my favorite men in the world. In one place. At the same exact time. With the exact same expression."

Eli went over to her, stroked her hair like he always did, and kissed her. "Hi, baby."

He moved out of the way so Galen could fit in the little space beside her bed. Galen kissed her forehead, then stood up. "Hey there, sis. What did you have that was good for lunch?"

Lena rolled her eyes. "They didn't bring me lunch yet. Is that why you're here? To steal my lunch?"

Galen laughed. "Maybe …" Then he moved away so Hunter and William could each take their turn in the little space beside Lena. They each hugged her and kissed her on the cheek.

Lena decided to hide her suspicion for now. These days, she didn't trust her emotions one bit. "I'm so glad you all came to visit me. I get to go home Sunday. I'm nervous, but relieved. My liver is behaving itself, and my kidney is almost doing the same."

Eli reluctantly sat in a chair down from her bed. "That's really great, sweetheart. I can't wait to have you home."

The rest of the men looked around.

Lena knew that her suspicions were correct. Her heart wasn't playing tricks on her. "Um, boys? You gonna tell me what this is all about? Oh no! Not Mama! She hasn't been here in a few days and—"

Galen interrupted her. "No, Lena. It's not Mama. She just caught a cold and didn't want to give it to you. Gracie was supposed to tell you that."

Lena sighed with relief. "Oh, no. Well, Gracie isn't the most reliable person unless it's in *Entertainment Weekly*. She probably forgot. Is she doing okay?"

Galen laughed nervously. "Yeah. Probably. It's just a little cold. Still, she didn't want to take her chances." Lena nodded, satisfied by the answer.

Lena looked from man to man. They were all looking anywhere but at her. They were obviously unnerved, which made Lena impatient. "Well?"

Finally, she looked at Galen, who opened his mouth twice, then closed it, obviously looking for the right words. "Oh, Galen, for crying out loud. Just spit it out!"

"It's Myrna."

Lena could feel the tears well up in her eyes. She could start crying in a second, lately.

"Is she sick? Did you call a vet?"

Galen turned toward the window, tears in his eyes as well. He thought he could do it, but he was not a heartbreaker, especially when it came to Lena.

William stepped up to where Galen was and took Lena's hand. He crouched down on his knees and smoothed her hair. "Sweetie, Myrna died."

The tears flowed for Lena's horse that had been her best friend more than anyone else. The horse that had taken her places when she needed to escape the twins and the pain of Daddy's death. Myrna had been there through it all. Lena had talked to Myrna like she was her best friend and Myrna had listened. She was the most loyal friend Lena had in this world and Lena had been absent when Myrna needed her most. When Myrna died, it was supposed to be Lena's face she saw before she took her last breath as well as Lena's voice as the last words she heard. There was no goodbye, nor was there the reassurance that Lena loved her.

Lena's voice was hoarse and cracked. "How?"

She was choking out words through her tears now.

William looked at her with sad eyes and continued to stroke her hair.

"She was being lunged to settle her down after her accident. There was a trap meant for Zars set in the mud."

Lena's tears were flowing like a fountain. "Oh, Myrna. Lame?"

William's eyes started to tear up now. Hunter took the weight from him and continued the story.

"The vet said she was in enormous pain. I … made sure she didn't suffer anymore."

Lena nodded in approval. William moved out of the tiny place where it was possible to be near Lena, allowing Eli to replace him. He pulled Lena into a hug and allowed her to cry into his chest. The other men kissed her cheek and left, feeling helpless. Each one had tears falling down his own cheeks. Lena spent the night mourning yet another loss as Eli steadied her.

CHAPTER 27

"Mind if I come in?" Nurse Smiley knocked on Lena's door a little later than usual. Lena was grateful. After the night she'd just had, she welcomed the opportunity to sleep in.

"Hi, Rebecca. Of course. Please come in."

Rebecca and Lena had become fast friends. Rebecca Smiley had been Lena's only respite during this whole nightmare. She seemed to understand Lena and was able to talk to her like no one else could. Lena was comfortable with Rebecca. It was like Rebecca was a sister that understood her more than her own.

Rebecca liked Lena, too. Rebecca's childhood had not been a good one, but she had persevered. Lena's story intrigued her. Rebecca had lost a sister early in her life and Lena was taking over the empty space in her heart.

Rebecca barely made her way into the room when there was another knock at the door.

"Shall I get that?"

Lena sighed. "Only if you promise not to leave. So many visitors. I'd rather just sit here and hang out with just you."

Rebecca made an imaginary cross sign over her heart. "Cross my heart."

Rebecca opened the door to a very suave Hunter. He'd cleaned up and looked ruggedly handsome. He was wearing a pair of jeans and a brown corduroy sports jacket. Under the sports jacket was a tight green T-shirt that brought out his velvet brown eyes. His hair was combed for once and he smelled heavenly, stepping into the room with a bouquet of flowers.

Lena couldn't believe her eyes. "Whoa!"

Rebecca started to stammer. "Uh … hi. I'm the nurse … uh, Lena's nurse! Well, not at this exact moment. But, at other exact moments I am. I'm just her friend … who's a nurse … but I'm also her friend when I *am* a nurse … That's not her nurse … Right now …"

Lena just smiled. "Um, excuse me? Friend that's not my nurse, but just a nurse? Can you invite my brother into the room, please?"

Rebecca's cheeks flushed. "Oh! Yes. Sorry. Please, come in!"

Hunter was amused and Lena could see a devilish grin spread across his face. Rebecca was in jeans as well. Skinny jeans, which made Lena jealous. They made her legs look ten feet tall. Her hair was in perfect black ringlets that danced all over her head. The little gold specks in her brown eyes twinkled, and her cinnamon skin was perfect as usual. Her unusually long eyelashes fluttered everywhere. If Lena didn't love her so much, she would probably hate her for being so gorgeous.

Hunter was obviously as struck by Rebecca. Lena didn't usually believe in love at first sight, but this was certainly a perfect example.

"I'm Hunter … who is her brother but wasn't her brother … because we only have the same father … so I'm currently her brother, who wasn't always her brother, but is currently."

Hunter gave Rebecca a wicked smile. It was the first time Lena had seen this flirtatious side of Hunter. It was also the first time Lena had felt playful and fun since her accident.

"Do you two need a moment or something?" Lena asked, chuckling as she spoke.

Rebecca looked back at Lena, then to Hunter. "Oh my. What would I do with a moment? I think I've already messed up my first impression beautifully."

Hunter just snickered. "On the contrary. I find you to be delightful and a breath of fresh air."

Lena looked at Hunter. "Why are you all dressed up?"

Hunter handed the flowers to Lena. "First, these are for you."

Lena took them, smelled them, then handed them to Rebecca to put on the windowsill with all her other collectibles.

"I'm afraid I have bad news. For me. You will find it amusing, I'm sure." Hunter was over-pronouncing his words, obviously setting up his humorous scenario for Lena.

"Yes, I'd like to hear this."

Hunter rolled his eyes and returned to his normal enunciation. "Fine. I've been asked to be a part of the Butler Fair and Agricultural Association. I have a meeting this evening."

Lena couldn't believe her ears. "The Butler County Fair? You are going to be a part of the board that runs the big Butler County Fair? Hunter, that's awesome!"

Hunter grinned. "And ... I have to dress like this for meetings."

Lena saw her opportunity and she just had to tease him a little bit. "Hmmmm ... I don't know."

Hunter looked at her in surprise. "What! What's wrong?"

Lena tapped her finger on her chin as if she were looking him over. She winked at Rebecca when he wasn't looking. "No. This won't do, Hunter. You can't go to a board meeting like this."

Hunter was obviously shocked. "Why not? What's wrong?" Hunter curled his head around to look behind him as if his jacket were ripped. Then he began inspecting himself for stains, etc.

Rebecca caught on and got in the fun. "Oh yes. I see the problem."

Hunter looked at them in horror. "I don't have time to change? What's wrong!" Hunter was still inspecting himself. Rebecca found her mind going to erotic places.

Lena looked at Rebecca. "Well? We will just have to send him like this and hope for the best."

A horrified Hunter looked at them. "Please! Tell me what's wrong! This is my first meeting."

Lena went first. "No hat."

Then Rebecca chimed in. "No tie."

Hunter grabbed his head and his neck instantaneously. "Oh my gosh. I didn't even think about that! Do you think I have time—"

Lena and Rebecca roared with laughter. Hunter suddenly looked at them in disgust. "Are you kidding me?" Then he joined in the joke himself. "Okay. Very funny, ladies. Ha-ha."

When they all settled down, Lena got back into bed. Hunter kissed her on the head. "Now that I'm late!" Lena just smiled. He went to exit but turned back and went over to Rebecca. He took her hand and kissed it slowly, pausing for a moment before returning it. He stared directly into her eyes before he spoke. He spoke very softly and deliberately. "It was so nice to meet you."

Rebecca flushed red. "So ... nice to meet you. Lena's brother." Hunter flashed a killer smile. Rebecca hoped her cheeks were slightly less red than she imagined.

"And, sister? It was so nice to hear you laugh again."

Lena smiled back at him. "It was so nice to laugh again, Hunter, even if at your expense."

Hunter smiled back. "If that's what it takes, so be it." With that, he turned and walked out the door.

For the rest of the visit, Rebecca settled down and she and Lena had a wonderful time. Lena decided that playing matchmaker with Rebecca and Hunter would make for a great distraction.

CHAPTER 28

Galen walked into the barn as Eli was putting away Venus, one of the younger racehorses he was trying to train. "How are her times?"

Eli chuckled. "Times? I think what you'd like to ask me is can I get her around a racetrack one time without being distracted by the occasional squirrel or chipmunk."

Galen winced. He knew Venus was fast and had good lines, but going in the right direction was paramount.

Eli put Venus away and went to his truck, pulling out a clean shirt. Galen stumbled over his words. "Oh, a clean shirt … because you're dirty …"

Eli looked at him weirdly. "I guess so?"

Galen sighed. This was not going the way he wished. "You're changing your shirt to bring Lena home from the hospital, right?"

Eli still felt this was a weird conversation. "Would you rather I wear the dirty, stinky one?" Eli just looked at him in shock, wondering if Galen noticed the awkward nature of this conversation.

"No. Of course not. I … just wondered if you wouldn't mind a change of plans." Eli still looked at him like he was an alien from another planet. "Oh, this is the most awkward conversation I've had in a while. Let me try a do-over."

Eli was still looking at him with big eyes. "Yes. Please!"

Galen motioned for Eli to walk over to the fence with him. Gale jumped up and sat on the fence. Eli smiled to himself, remembering how much Lena used to do that all the time. "Something funny?"

Eli just smiled. "No. Please. I'm sorry."

Galen proceeded. "So ... would you mind terribly if I were to bring Lena home today?"

Eli looked at Galen suspiciously. "You?"

Galen shrugged. "I miss her, too." Eli still just looked at him. "Look. There's nothing weird going on, I swear. There is just something I need to talk to her about, brother to sister. I promise, once I get her home, she's all yours, Eli."

Eli looked at him with suspicion. "Okay. But Lena and I need to be together the next couple of days, Galen. We need time to put ourselves back together."

Galen hopped off the fence and put his hand on his shoulder. "Eli, I totally understand that. You will get no complaints from me. I promise."

Galen turned to walk away before Eli called his name, causing him to turn back around. "Yes?"

Eli walked over to him. "Please drop her off at the hayfield above the house when you come home."

Galen nodded and proceeded to his car, putting the top down, knowing Lena loved it.

Galen entered the hospital room slowly. Lena looked confused but hopped up and hugged Galen anyways. "Where's Eli?"

Gale sat down on the bed. "I asked him if I could bring you home."

"Why?"

"Well, there's something that I want to talk to you about, but I wanted to do it on the way home."

Interrupting, the discharge nurse came in with Lena's papers. "You have an appointment with the doctor next week. Don't miss it. If you have any problems before then, please don't hesitate to come in. Your kidney function is not perfect, but the doctor says you've been here long enough. She's happy with it enough to let you go. But please. No. Alcohol. And follow the diet as prescribed."

Lena looked at the nurse and waved her hands. "You can count on it. I promise." The nurse nodded, handed her the papers, and left.

Galen just put up his hands. "Great."

Lena looked at him, surprised. "What?"

Galen said in a teasing voice, "That was my plan. To stop at the saloon and get you all liquored up. Now what am I going to do?"

Lena smacked his arm playfully. "Come on. Let's go. I've spent enough time in here!"

Galen took her bags and Lena hopped into the wheelchair. "Is this really necessary?" she pleaded with the previous nurse.

"Hospital policy."

Galen just laughed. "Well, I'll go ahead of you and get the car."

The nurse just smiled. "Your boyfriend is nice, Ms. Maleno. Attractive, too, if I might say so."

Lena made a barfing sound. "Nurse! That is my brother!"

The nurse stopped and looked at her, horrified. "Oh! I'm so sorry."

Lena pretended not to be secretly proud.

"Your chariot awaits."

Lena giggled and got into the passenger seat. "Thank you, Galen!"

The nurse waved goodbye and they were off.

On the way home, they chatted, although it was apparent that Lena was quite nervous.

"What's wrong?"

Lena just sighed. "I'm just nervous. I don't want to be everyone's charity case, Galen."

Galen sighed this time. "Lena, that's not how it is."

"I don't really want to talk about it."

Galen decided to let it go. Instead, he pulled up a long, winding road that led to a charming little cottage. When he stopped, Lena got out of the car. "Oh. I forgot about this place! Galen. How did you remember this?"

Gale smiled. "It's Grandma and Grandpa's. Do you think I could forget the one place I could get free peppermint candy whenever I wanted it?"

Lena ran up the porch. "Yes. I remember. Grandma's rocker! I can't believe it's still here on the porch."

Galen smiled again. "I inherited it."

Lena looked at him. "You inherited Grandma and Grandpa's cottage? That's so sweet!"

Galen looked out over the banister. "Is it? I pretty much live in Pittsburgh, Lena. What am I going to do with this broken-down old cottage?"

Lena went over to him. "Broken down? Oh, Galen! How could you call this sweet place broken down! I admit it needs some TLC. But there is a lot of love here. A lot of memories." Lena sat in the rocker and looked around. "You mean this is all yours? You don't have to share with Mama or any of us?"

Galen looked at her again. "No. I think Daddy knew that ..."

Lena looked away, realizing what he meant to say. She finished his sentence. "That you were the one true Maleno?"

Galen was ashamed and instantly defensive. He honestly thought that was why his father left this place to just him. "I don't want it."

Lena looked at him. "Galen! You could use this as a summer home."

Galen laughed. "Isn't that why I come to the ranch?"

Lena just looked at him. "I guess so ..."

They were quiet for a moment. Then, Lena tried again. "Galen. This is where we came to visit our grandparents. Why would you want to sell it? It's so darling."

Galen looked at her. "I don't want to sell it."

Lena looked confused. "Okay, I'm totally not with you on this, Galen."

Galen turned her to look at him. "I want to give it to you, Lena."

Lena backed down the stairs. "Oh no. No, you don't, Galen. I don't want you just handing me houses because I've fallen on rough times! No way! That's not how this is going to work!"

Galen stopped her. "That's not why I'm giving it to you."

That piqued Lena's interest enough to stop and look at him quizzically. "Okay. Why?"

Galen had to choose his words carefully. Lena was strong-willed and not likely to accept a handout. "Free room and board."

Lena just laughed. "What? That's insane."

Galen powered through. "No! It isn't. I don't have time for a place like this, but you and Eli are starting out in life. And I know you, Lena. You will love a place like this. You will both fix it up and make it a home. It's Grandpa's place. It should stay in our family. I want to come and stay here when I need to rest. I don't want to worry about paying taxes and water pipes freezing and heating this and windows and—"

Lena stopped him. "Okay. I get it. But we need to pay you something for it."

Galen just looked at her. "A room that's mine, a key, and a home-cooked meal every once in a while. When the ranch house is full of ... well, ranch drama ... just let me come here. Just let me rest."

Lena had tears in her eyes. "Are you sure? Galen, you are giving me a house!"

Galen laughed. "I'm giving you a broken-down, fixer-upper cottage. There's a difference."

Lena looked wistfully at the cottage. "Not to me, Gale. Not to me."

Galen opened the door. "We better go."

"Do we have to? Can't I just stay in my house?"

Galen laughed. "I'll draw up papers tomorrow. Once they go through, then it will be your house."

Lena smiled. It was the first time Galen had seen her smile like that in an awfully long time. "You're going to repaint it yellow. Tell me I'm wrong."

Lena laughed heartily. "You know me so well, Gale!" She hugged him one last time, thanked him, and got back in the car, waiting for Galen to proceed with their trip.

Galen told Lena about dropping her off at the hayfield. "Why?"

"I don't know, Lena. I just do as the man asks."

Closer to the house, she could see everyone on the porch, awaiting her arrival. "Gale, can't you just take me straight to Eli?"

"Just say hello. Best to rip off the Band-Aid, Lena."

Galen stopped, and Lena departed the convertible like she was a bride. Everyone had formed a receiving line for her.

"So glad you're home!" Lois was the first to greet her.

"It wasn't the same without you." In Lena's head, she was wondering if that was truly how William felt.

"You should see Zars now!" Bringing up Zars made her think about Myrna. She quickly put the thought out of her head and plastered on her fake smile and nod. *Smile and nod, Lena. Smile and nod.*

"We can't wait to show you!" *Sheesh. Allie and Dirk have a one-track mind!*

"You look beautiful." *Okay, so Hunter started out as a creep, but ended up being cool!*

"Who wants another makeover?" *Oh no. Gracie, please. Not another makeover.*

"I love your outfit! Trés chic, little sister!" *Uh, really? Jean shorts and my favorite blue top?*

Lena's head was spinning. She turned and set off to run away, and ran straight into Eli, who scooped her into a hug.

"Mind if I borrow our homecoming queen?"

Without waiting for an answer, he carried Lena up the little hill and put her in his truck, where they rode to the scene of the accident.

Lena began to panic. "Eli! I don't want to come here!"

Eli pulled the truck over, reaching for her hand. He patted it and emerged from the truck, walking to her side. He opened the creaky door and took Lena by the hand.

"Lena, what do you do when you fall off a horse?"

Lena looked at him with panic-stricken eyes. "Get right back on ... but Eli!" She could see where this was going. "I didn't just fall off a horse."

Eli put his hand against her cheek and stroked her bottom lip. "Lena. I love you. More than anything in this whole entire world, I love you. You don't ever have to face anything alone, ever again. We need to face this. Together. It's going to hurt. But the difference is that we are here for each other. Do you still love me?"

Lena's looked at him with soulful eyes. "Oh, Eli! Of course, I love you. And ... I trust you."

Eli held out his hand. "Well?" Lena reluctantly took it.

The healing journey Eli had in mind began not far from where they stood.

He walked her over to a pile of stones where two horseshoes made the letter M on a mounted stick. Lena sat by the rock pile and began to cry as she touched Myrna's horseshoes. Slowly, she knelt and brushed her hands over the dirt that covered her beloved horse. Eli stood right behind her but gave her enough room to sever the lasting bond between her and Myrna.

"I wasn't here for her! She was here for everything and I wasn't here for her! Oh, Myrna!" Lena threw herself on the grave and allowed herself to sob.

Eli just sat with her and allowed her to grieve. She needed time with Myrna that was just hers. Although it cut him like a knife, he told himself that he had to be strong.

Finally, she had done all the crying she could. She hugged Eli and buried her head in his chest. When she picked her head up, she could see something in a faraway tree.

Lena squinted her eyes. At first, she thought it was just the tears clouding her vision. "What ..."

She moved toward the tree for a closer look to find that Eli had carved a cross into the tree and mounted another horseshoe. Under the cross were the words "Beloved Baby Miller."

Lena touched the words and ran into Eli's arms. "You are the most wonderful man in the whole world, Eli Miller."

Eli and Lena just sat there for hours, healing.

CHAPTER 29

Lena felt peaceful on her way back to the ranch. She no longer felt like people were walking on eggshells around her, as before, but rather like they were just trying to love her.

Dirk walked over and spoke in a quiet voice. "Hey, Lena. If you have a minute, we would like you to come with us." She could see that behind Dirk's truck was a horse trailer, with Zars. Allie was in riding gear.

"We thought you might be up to watching a little racing."

Lena looked at Dirk with bright eyes. "Seriously?"

Dirk looked pleased with her response. "Well, we are just taking him out. He is not actually racing anyone. We have been taking him out quite a bit lately."

Lena seemed excited. "Let's go!" She was ready for the distraction. Although she could never forget what she had just been through, she had to start replacing a lot of pain with new memories, which meant she had to start living again.

Lena loved listening to Dirk and Allie laugh, joke, and tell stories. It was obvious how much they loved each other.

Allie almost squealed when they pulled up to the racetrack. "I've been waiting for this day for so long!"

Lena chuckled. "What do you mean?"

Allie turned around in the passenger seat to face Lena and suddenly turned profoundly serious. "For so long, I've never felt like I fit into this family. I feel like this is my time!"

Lena looked apologetic. "Allie, I'm so sorry you felt that way. I never wanted you to feel left out. You have such a kind soul."

Allie had a newfound strength about her. She was not dwelling on the past. "Hey. I get it. Between the twins, then you and Galen ... It's hard to be the middle child. But now the middle child is gonna knock all your socks off!"

They pulled into the track, and Allie and Dirk went to prepare. Lena just walked around, nostalgic.

She remembered Daddy taking her here and how much she loved his excitement. She remembered how much he used to teach her about horses, jockeys, and racing.

As she walked up to the edge of the track beside an older gentleman with a cane, tears flooded her eye as she whispered, "Oh, Daddy. I miss you."

A deep, husky voice came from the gentleman with the cane. "We all do."

Lena looked intently at the man, who was dark-skinned and had gray hair, smiling as she discovered who it was. "Mr. Scotts!" Mr. Scotts nodded, and Lena hugged him. "I can't believe it's really you!"

Mr. Scotts sighed. "It is. Your mother contacted me not long ago."

Lena looked confused. "Mama? Why?"

Mr. Scotts held Lena's hand while they found a place on the bleachers. He had certainly aged. "You don't give your mother credit. You don't think she knows Allie is the jockey on that huge racehorse of yours?"

Lena felt a little foolish. Mother really does know best.

"Your daddy taught you all about horses and racing, but he did not teach you about racetracks. It can be a complicated game here, Ms. Helena. You could lose your shirt."

Lena's plan had been to attend this race with Dirk and Allie for fun. Her head was not ready for talk of complicated games and losing her shirt. However, Mr. Scotts was wise, and she wanted to make the most of the opportunity for his free advice, so she listened intently.

"Your daddy had a knack for all of this. He had a sixth sense about horses. Your mama says you have that gift as well. But your daddy had fire. I would come here with him to make sure he didn't get his tongue twisted, resulting in him having his face rearranged."

Lena felt slightly guilty for having been amused by that comment. Mr. Scotts always had a colorful way of expressing himself.

"Thank you for taking care of him, Mr. Scotts."

Mr. Scotts proceeded. "Oh, no need to thank me. He taught me about horses along with you. I'm a rich man!"

Lena looked down at the pavement, as did Mr. Scotts.

"I miss him, too."

At that moment, Dirk came out of the gate with an exceptionally large Zars and a very tiny Allie, causing Mr. Scotts to shake his head.

Lena was suddenly worried. "Is something wrong?"

Mr. Scotts looked at Lena. "If Zars is ready to race, Allie will be the tiniest jockey out there."

Lena knew what he was thinking. Allie looked like a porcelain doll on that massive horse.

As they walked by Lena and Mr. Scotts, Allie turned her head in pride. There was no taking this moment away from Allie. It would take ten thousand men to pull her from that horse.

"Mr. Scotts! It's so nice to see you! What a coincidence you are here to see our Zars race!"

Lena and Mr. Scotts looked at each other, then broke out into a chuckle.

"I consider it an honor, Allie."

Allie was all smiles.

Dirk got Zars into a starting position and Allie situated herself. Dirk rang a makeshift bell and Zars took off.

He had been a god of a horse from the day Daddy got him. Thinking for a moment of how beautiful Zars looked, there was something that impressed Lena even more.

It was tiny Allie, who was a pillar of strength. This massive, beautiful animal was relying on this tiny person to make him perform at his best!

Lena and Mr. Scotts were on the edge of their seats when Zars and Allie reached the finish line. Mr. Scotts clicked his stopwatch and showed it to Lena, whose eyes got as big as silver dollars. "Is that ..."

Mr. Scotts looked down at his watch to be sure. "First time out, and he broke the track record."

Lena was dumbfounded. "Well. If you'll help me, Mr. Scott, I believe we have something here!"

Mr. Scotts nodded in approval. "Let's race him in two days. Give him a day of rest. Get your family on board."

Suddenly there was another voice behind her. "How about racing him against someone?"

Lena turned around while rolling her eyes. She was in no mood for William today. "Such as?"

William said simply, "Snow."

"The horse we gave Hunter? He can't possibly be ready!"

William chuckled. "Oh, he's not, but he needs to get on a track for once. And we need to see where we need to work. We need to see how the jockey is working out and how he races."

Lena looked confused, but William rambled on.

"I have no doubt Zars will win, but it will be a good test. I've already scheduled a race here for 1 p.m. on Wednesday."

Lena shook her head. She thought this was crazy for William, but she was agreeable. "Okay, then."

Allie squealed. "Yay! More racing!"

Dirk just shook his head. It was apparent that he thought this idea was crazy, but he agreed as well. "We will be here."

Mr. Scotts, always the gentleman, put his hat into the ring. "So shall I."

Lena was grateful for something that kept her mind from everything else.

She picked up her bag and was just about to leave when she noticed something out of the corner of her eye. "HEY!"

It was a man in a hoodie walking around them. He had bumped into her, which made her suspicious. The track was nowhere close to crowded. "That guy that went through the gate!"

William and Dirk jogged after him but returned.

"He just vanished!" Dirk reported.

Something was amiss, and Lena was determined to find out what it was.

CHAPTER 30

Lena arose that morning after a night of little sleep. There was an uneasy feeling surrounding the race from the day before that refused to leave her thoughts. She quickly headed downstairs for breakfast, where Lois and Galen were discussing the race. It was the hottest topic these days.

Lois heard the creaking steps and looked up at Lena, who was rubbing her eyes. "Good morning! I thought you would sleep a little longer."

Lena looked puzzled. "Why?"

Lois looked at her, startled that she had no recollection of her sleeping habits from the previous night. "You were up and down all night!"

Lena just shook it off and changed the subject. "Oh. So. Mama."

"Yes?" Lois answered nonchalantly while making pancakes.

"The funniest thing happened when we went to the track yesterday. Guess who was there?" Lena was using a very overly dramatic tone. Galen was obviously enjoying the conversation. Lena could see Lois' eyes dance.

Lois decided to play coy, much to Lena's dismay. "It's a racetrack, dear. Absolutely anyone could be there!" Then she huffed as if Lena had just asked the silliest question and was interrupting her pancake-making.

Galen was amused but bewildered at the same time. "As usual, I'm obviously confused."

Lena looked over at him. "Oh, Galen. Allow me to clue you in. Mr. Scotts, Daddy's oldest and dearest friend, just happened to be at the racetrack. He showed up on the day that Daddy's most prized horse was out for the first time. He also just happened to know who the jockey on that horse was. Isn't that so ironic?" Lena was using that overly dramatic voice again.

Galen did not understand Lena's cynical nature. According to him, it was the best coincidence ever. "Mr. Scotts? No way! I haven't seen him since Daddy's funeral."

Lois started humming and singing to herself as if she had no clue there was a conversation going on behind her. Lena just looked at her skeptically. "Oh, Mama?"

Lois answered her in a sing-songy voice. "Why yes, dear?"

Lena was finished with this entire skit. "Mama. Mr. Scotts told me you called."

Lois got very antsy, turning suddenly after putting the pancakes on Galen's plate. Her movements were very rigid. "Galen, will you give us a minute?"

Galen was annoyed. "What? But I just put the butter and syrup on! It'll get cold!"

Lois was frustrated this time. "Well, it's nice outside. Here's your apple juice. Go outside and eat."

Galen stomped outside like a six-year-old. He turned back around just as Lois slammed the door in his face.

Just then, the twins entered. Gracie sighed. "Mama, we have nothing to wear to this race tomorrow!"

Charlie was much happier. "Well, we don't know that! What does one wear to a race? Do we need to go shopping, Mama?"

Galen poked his head through the kitchen window. He was finished with his pancakes. "Mama, I'm finished. I'm coming back in."

Lena laughed. He really was a six-year-old sometimes.

As he entered, he handed his mother the plate. "Girls, this isn't an actual horse race ..." He thought for a moment, then went to the bottom of the stairs. "Oh come on."

Charlie stopped him. "Where are we going?"

Galen pulled her to the stairs. "To see what you brought with you, of course!"

Charlie started up the stairs after him. "Seriously? Best. Brother. Ever." She said it excitedly and pronounced each word with her hands.

Galen just brushed it off. "Yeah, yeah."

After everyone left, Lois turned her attention to Lena again.

"I don't want to step on your toes, but this is Allie's big day. She has never been so excited before. Lena, you know a lot about—"

Lena interrupted. She could see where this conversation was going, so she stopped it before Lois continued with the wrong idea.

"Mama, you are totally misunderstanding me."

Lois stopped in shock. Lena chuckled before she began again. "I don't want to scold you. I'm really just teasing you. We all love Mr. Scotts, and we have since we were children. I have no problem with his involvement."

Lois looked up from the towel she was wringing in her hands and smiled. She wanted to carefully plant her next question without upsetting Lena.

"How are you, Lena? I mean, really." Lois reached out her hand and grabbed an unprepared Lena's while she asked.

Lena sighed at the question everyone had been so afraid to ask.

Lena thought long and hard before giving her an answer. She wanted to be sincere about her response.

"I'm honestly okay, Mother. One step at a time. I'm moving through life with caution. I feel like Galen!"

Lois tossed her head back and let out a hearty laugh and Lena joined in, not noticing Galen coming down the stairs and into the kitchen. "What are you two laughing about?"

They both started to laugh even harder. Galen was bewildered. "What's so funny?" He stomped out of the kitchen and pouted in his recliner.

Eli cautiously walked in while everyone was giggling. "Uh … I'm sorry to break up the party …"

Galen bolted out of his recliner. "Eli! Yes. Thank you so much for coming when you did! The estrogen in this house is driving everyone mad."

Laughing, Eli sauntered over and kissed Lena before he answered. "Well, we can't have that, now, can we!" He looked at Lena. "Are you going crazy with estrogen?"

Lena just huffed. "Who are you going to believe. Me or Galen?"

Eli just put up his hands. "Oh no. I'm not dumb enough to answer that question!" He kissed her forehead, then walked over to playfully jab at Galen. Lois yelled at them for roughhousing, and Lena pretended to laugh that Galen was in trouble, as if they were kids again.

No one saw Hunter enter.

"Is Dad here?"

Everyone spun around and looked at the door where Hunter had entered, shocked to hear Hunter refer to William as "Dad." Everyone froze awkwardly. The twins came bubbling down, talking a mile a minute, but stopped when they saw everyone frozen in the kitchen.

Charlie, always the sibling to say the most inappropriate thing at the most inappropriate time, thought her talents would be suitable at this moment. "Someone die?"

Lois looked daggers at Charlie as Lena was still raw about such comments. Eli answered her question. "No, Hunter just asked for William."

The look on Hunter's face spoke volumes. He was unsure whether to leave, stay, speak, or stay silent.

Charlie also had a knack for saying the most appropriate things at the most appropriate moments as well. It was a very weird talent to possess. "Oh! William just pulled up in the truck, Hunter. Better go get him before he roams around somewhere else!"

There was no hesitation from Hunter. He backed out of the doorway and ran down the porch steps three at a time.

Everyone began filing out of the kitchen to start their day. Before Lena knew it, it was almost time for the race.

CHAPTER *31*

Everyone was so happy to see Mr. Scotts at the track. He had visited often until his wife became ill with Alzheimer's Disease. Lena remembered that he always had licorice on him. She loved that memory as a child.

Suddenly, another guest showed up that no one recognized. No one except Lena that is.

"Over here!" Lena waved at a tall, gorgeous, graceful woman. Her head was wrapped in a gorgeous paisley scarf where the most beautiful ringlet curls stuck out of the back. She was well put-together and had dark skin and long eyelashes. The twins thought instantly that she was a model. The girl waved back at Lena and started over toward the group. Lena secretly grinned at the thought of Charlie being jealous and intimidated by someone else's beauty.

Rebecca Smiley was not only beautiful when she was searching the crowd for her friend, but she was even more gorgeous when she was smiling. It had nothing to do with her last name. She was beautiful inside and out. It was no wonder that Lena had taken to her instantly as a best friend.

"Everyone? This is Rebecca Smiley. She was my nurse in the ICU and now she is my best friend." Lena hugged Rebecca as they sat beside each other. Rebecca beamed with pride.

Charlie was quiet at first, which made Lena slightly suspicious. However, Charlie was trying hard lately to change, and Lena was proud of her.

"I just love your shoes! Are they Jimmy Choo?"

Rebecca looked down at her shoes and modeled her foot. "I am afraid they are BOGO. Payless!"

Charlie just nodded confusedly. Lena could tell she had no idea what Rebecca just said. "BOGO? I don't know him ..."

Rebecca tried to look sweet, but the look on her face was shocked. She had no idea whether Charlie was being serious or just messing with her, so she decided to just drop it.

Finally, the horses came out onto the racetrack. Gracie addressed her mother frantically. "Mama. Allie is late! Seriously. I've texted her a million times. I don't know what's happened to her!"

Charlie suddenly joined in the melee. "She is never late! That's it. I'm going to look for her."

Lois needed an excuse. The girls had no idea that Allie was the jockey for this event, and the time had not come yet for them to know. "Um, ladies, it's fine. Allie is asleep. She caught some sort of stomach bug and is not feeling well. I told her to lie down and if she was feeling well later, to come on down. If she didn't, I told her not to worry, we would know she was still in bed."

Charlie and Gracie looked shocked at first. Allie normally attended every important event, no matter how she felt. They got over it quickly as the horses pulled up to the gate.

Galen squinted. "The jockey on Zars is so small compared to the jockey on Snowglider! It's so weird! Small jockey on a giant horse, big jockey on a tiny horse. How about that!"

Lois chuckled nervously. "Yes. How about that." She just winced at Lena. Allie looked completely fragile on Zars, but Lena knew better.

The horses were ready, and the bell sounded. Zars leapt out of the gate and ran down the track, making Allie look like she could fly.

Snowglider kept pace at the first few lengths but soon fell back. Snow was still young and was not favored to win this race, or any other for a while, but he had promise for the future.

Suddenly, Lena caught a flash of light on the final turn. It instantly put her into a trance.

A memory suddenly flashed through her head. Her mind saw the flash when she was on Myrna, racing Eli. It was the same flash, and she could almost feel Myrna rear. There was no time! Lena could feel a nightmare unfolding in front of her. All she could do was stand up and yell, "ALLIE!" But Allie was out of earshot, and Lena was unable to move. *Move, Lena, move! Get up!*

Allie was quick and fierce. Lena could see Allie try to slow Zars down, but he was going way too fast. Allie made a split decision and did the only thing she could. She turned Zars around and went the opposite direction.

Snowglider obediently followed. Eli was already on a dead run for the final turn when he saw the flash of light as well. Finally, everything made sense. He had been asking himself all these months why an expert rider like Lena would have panicked on her horse and why a horse as excellent as Myrna would suddenly rear and buck Lena. Now, his memory was not failing him any longer and he knew exactly what had happened. The flash of light had removed the block his subconscious had put on his memory.

Galen was confused as usual. "Can someone please tell me what is going on?"

Lena was pale as snow, unable to look away. Her adrenaline was pumping, and she could feel herself snapping out of her trance. Bolting up out of her seat like a jack-in-the-box, she could feel her throat open and the words coming out of her like a siren. "Someone is trying to throw Zars with the same flash that threw Myrna! On the last turn!" She pointed, and Galen squinted again. Suddenly, he could see it. Everyone could see the moment on his face when he realized what was going on.

Galen suddenly set off at a dead run for the final turn as well. Incapable of running in his expensive shoes, Galen let out a curse word, ripped them off, and ran the rest of the way in his equally as expensive socks.

Eli was the first to arrive at the turn. Lena could see him hop the fence and tackle someone in the hooded sweatshirt— the gentleman that had bumped into her at the track last time.

Lena shook herself out of what remained of her daze when she noticed the entire family started running for the fence. Allie took Zars back to the stable and the other jockey took Snowglider back.

By the time Lena got there, Galen had pulled Eli off the hooded man before he beat him to death. Shocked, Lena realized that he had never truly gotten over what happened to Lena or their child. It was all coming out like a geyser right now and it took everything Galen had inside of him to control Eli.

"*You almost killed her!!!*" Tears were streaming down Eli's face as he got in one last punch.

Lena could see the fury in Eli's eyes, so she went over and held him as he shook in her arms. She just held him and rubbed his back as he fell to the ground on his knees.

Over Eli's shoulder, she could see the fear in the eyes of his victim, who was not ready for this brand-new furious Eli Miller that no one knew existed. Not even Eli.

CHAPTER 32

Lena started to tear up, mostly because Eli was a mess, and it broke her heart. She was healing, and Eli was still being tormented, which made Lena feel selfish. He was so busy making sure Lena had healed that he had ignored himself. Eli stopped shaking and was able to stand. Lena went after the hooded man.

"Why? Why have you done this?"

Lena stepped back once she realized that she was looking straight into the bloody eyes of Derek Hopstef, whom she had suspected all along.

Derek spat out blood before he spat out his next contemptuous comment. "I don't owe you an explanation." He had grown so indifferent and devious. Lena knew that this evil and sinister man was no longer the normal Derek she had hired.

An angry, ferocious, almost superhuman Galen pulled Derek up with one hand and set him on his feet. He looked Derek straight in the eye with an animosity Lena never knew Galen carried. When he spoke, he sounded so vile, it scared her. "You are going to jail. Think of that as a gift. I had half a mind to pull Eli off you, then pick up where he left off, and I'm still thinking that sounds like a rather good option."

Derek and Galen stared each other down. Derek knew better than to run. After watching Eli, he knew he could not outrun him. He attempted to appeal to Galen's anger, not discerning that Galen's lawyer side would always supersede.

But Derek tried anyway. "Why would I go to jail? I just flashed a mirror. That's not a crime."

Galen stared him down, gathering what little composure he had left, but Eli went right for him. It was Lena that stepped in between them and put up her hand. Eli was almost unable to stop himself. She put her hand on Eli's cheek, showing him that it was okay. Then, she turned to Derek.

Lena decided to move right up to Derek and look him in the eye. She had to do this. This was the closure she needed and deserved. Taking a deep breath, she looked at Derek, her voice low and calm. "You say you love me, Derek? You caused my child to be taken from me."

Suddenly, there was a look of horror on his face, then a look of understanding. Eli and Galen's rage suddenly made sense. Derek had wanted to make a point, but he had never wanted to cause Lena so much unsurmountable pain. He wanted the Malenos to realize that life on the ranch was harder without him, and he wanted them to appreciate his value. Lena was supposed to yearn for his return. They had to fall on hard times to do that, which meant hurting Zars, but he did not want to cause Lena pain. Derek's heart broke, but that was not enough satisfaction for Lena.

Derek just whispered to her, "What? What are you talking about?"

"I was pregnant when I was thrown from Myrna, Derek."

Derek suddenly looked at Eli, who had tears in his eyes. Lois, who was standing beside Eli, comforted him by rubbing his arm. Although Derek wanted Eli to feel the pain of his absence, this had not been his plan for Eli, either. He was jealous, but Eli had never caused him harm. In fact, Eli had always treated him well enough.

Derek knew nothing he said could make a difference now. Lena continued.

"You took so much from me, but you didn't break me, Derek. I will never give you that satisfaction. When you sit in jail, please know this. I will still be with the man I genuinely love and who loves me. You will never be with me. It will be his arms around me, and it will be our bed that I will be sleeping in every night. It will never be yours."

The officer Lois called showed up at that moment. Derek turned and went willingly with the officer. The rest of the family agreed to follow and give statements as soon as they dropped off the horses.

Charlie just looked at everyone. "Allie sure missed an interesting day!"

Suddenly a voice from behind the group spoke up. "I hate when that happens."

Everyone turned around to see Allie and the other jockey, still in uniform.

"This is Tim. He's our cousin. Hunter's brother."

Everyone just stood there, shocked.

Gracie held out her hand. "Hi, Tim."

Galen walked into the middle of the family circle. "Wait. Allie. So, *you* were the jockey that saved Zars?"

Allie beamed. She had been waiting so long for this moment. Everyone else just looked at her in amazement. Lena had never been so proud.

"You could have gotten hurt!" Typical Galen.

Allie just laughed. "Galen, I'm fine."

Galen just pointed at Allie, then at his mother. It was obvious by the look on Lois' face that she knew.

Allie interrupted his moment of awe. "You are impressed by how good I am, aren't you, Galen?" Allie rocked back and forth on her heels, smiling proudly.

Galen just looked at her. "Uh … well … Yeah! To be honest!"

Lois suggested that Galen pick his jaw up off the ground, get washed up, and help everyone head for the station. He was still shaking his head in disbelief as he left.

CHAPTER 33

The Maleno family and everyone involved with the scene at the track began to trickle in. Thankfully, the atmosphere of the situation had become much less intense. Derek was in holding. Although no one was laughing or smiling, everyone seemed to be stable and just waiting for their turn.

Suddenly, the doors flew open and a frantic older woman flew in, looking very disheveled. The tall, very thin woman looked as if she had been working in a garden. She was wearing corduroy pants, old sneakers, and gardening gloves that had obviously been in planting soil. Her tight bun did not hide the dirt on her face. A blue windbreaker was the only clean thing she was wearing. Lena recognized Mrs. Hopstef, but she looked like she had aged ten years since she last saw her.

Mrs. Hopstef looked frantic as she ran past the Malenos, endlessly tapping on the glass window. An officer was taking his time, obviously gossiping with another officer.

"Excuse me!"

The officer just looked at her. "I will be with you in a moment."

Ruth Hopstef was too impatient for such nonsense. She was stressed to the max and was about to break. "You will be with me *now.*"

The look of obvious fury on her face caused the two officers to abruptly halt their conversation. The officer who oversaw the window took her seat and the gentleman she was talking to stood guard, obviously making sure there would be no scene. "I am the mother of Derek Hopstef. I have just been called and told that he is in custody. I will see him now."

The officer at the front desk, a small-framed yet lovely woman looked at the officer behind her, who nodded and went through a door. "Yes, ma'am. We will be with you in one moment, I promise."

Ruth regained her composure and was able to mutter, "Thank you." She walked past the Maleno family, and awkwardly found an empty seat as the family just smiled stiffly and waited.

Ruth Hopstef had always had a frigid demeanor. She had had a very rough upbringing and did not trust many. Her husband, Ethan, was a drunk and a gambler. Ruth did not lead a glamorous life, but Lois was always kind to her, knowing how she lived. There was a rumor once that Ethan Hopstef had abused Ruth physically before he was incarcerated for drugs. When he was released from prison, he took to alcohol then died of liver failure.

Lois went over and sat beside her, matriarch to matriarch. "Ruth, I'm so sorry. I—"

Ruth, unable to look at her, took off her gloves as if they were long silk gloves one would wear with a gown, and spat back, "Save it, Lois."

Lois stopped, dumbfounded.

Ruth Hopstef finished taking her gloves off, finger by finger, then folded them and gently put them in her purse. Thinking for a moment before she spoke, she looked at Lois while the entire family looked on. "I don't blame any of you. Derek was showing some unsettling signs of his father, which is why I sent him to work. He was gambling and getting abusive. I figured work would help him before he turned into Ethan. I thought he might see how the other half lives and want more for himself. And for me."

Lois grabbed her hand, no matter how much Ruth's eyes protested. She relented and allowed Lois to hold her hand as she continued. "I see that was wrong. Any pity you have for him or me will only make matters worse. The only thing that would make things better would be for you to send anyone my way that would be interested in my land and my house. The ranch itself is no longer working, but it could be again if anyone put work into it. It's time for me to leave all of this behind and move on."

Lena was in disbelief. Ruth was just going to walk away.

"Mrs. Hopstef, if I may. Derek has a problem! He needs your love and support right now."

Mrs. Hopstef very elegantly unbuttoned two buttons on her shirt and pulled away the scarf that was tied around her neck, revealing some very fresh, deep purple bruises. It looked like she had been close to strangulation.

"Helena, is it?"

Lena nodded cautiously.

"I am a small-framed woman, and I can no longer fight off a man like I once could. This is how my son behaves. His problems are far more than I can bear any longer. This past weekend he almost killed me. He may be welcome once he pays his consequence and I no longer fear him. That remains to be seen. Right now, he hurts people. His time here is what is safest for everyone. I must make a choice. My life or his. If he kills me, he is going to end up here anyway. The only difference is, he will kill someone much more innocent in the process."

A detective came out of the room and took everyone's statements. A different officer took Mrs. Hopstef back to see Derek.

The detective spoke to the group collectively when he finished. "We will hold him for twenty-four hours on conspiracy. Mrs. Hopstef will have to take him into her custody because of his violent nature that one of you reported. Someone also felt he was a flight risk; therefore, he will relinquish his passport and his driver's license until his hearing. That should make it easier for Mrs. Hopstef to take him into custody."

"I will be doing no such thing." Ruth Hopstef entered the room behind Detective Rhine.

Detective Rhine, a young man in his thirties, turned around and looked at her in surprise.

"I will not be looking after Derek. I just told him goodbye. That will be all."

Detective Rhine had obviously not had this experience before. "But, Mrs. Hopstef, it could be weeks before his trial!"

Mrs. Hopstef remained cool and calm. "I understand. This is a hard decision. I will not be returning. I will put the money from his bank account into this account so that he may get necessities to help him survive here. I will be unavailable to help him after that. I would like you to begin the process of issuing a Protection from Abuse order for the Malenos if they so allow."

Detective Rhine replied very quietly and slowly. "Yes, ma'am, we just signed all of the paperwork. That is now in place. What about you?"

Mrs. Hopstef nodded. "It will be impossible for him to find me. Now, if I am no longer needed, you have my number.

I will be closing a bank account tomorrow morning and coming here only to transfer his money. My ranch will be going into the hands of a realtor by lunchtime tomorrow, and I will be leaving the state."

Detective Rhine still looked bewildered, as did the Malenos. "Will you leave a forwarding address, Mrs. Hopstef?"

Mrs. Hopstef almost choked out her answer. "No. I will not, and Derek's number will be blocked from my phone. He is on his own, and if you intend to find me, I will move again. I told him if he got into any trouble, I would not be helping him. I have seen my life flash before my eyes way too many times, Detective Rhine. I watched his father die because I tried to save him numerous times. I no longer have the emotional stability for this any longer. If that makes me cold and iron-hearted, so be it. If you'll excuse me."

Detective Rhine nodded. "Yes, ma'am. Good luck to you."

With that, Ruth Hopstef nodded to the stunned Maleno family and walked out the door.

CHAPTER *34*

Lena could feel a lot of emotions raging through her on the ride back from the station. The first was relief that no one would be sabotaging the ranch anymore. She was finally free and would no longer have to look over her shoulder. She also felt guilt. Was she somewhat responsible for Derek spiraling out of control? Maybe she should have stopped it. Did she egg him on? Maybe she should have fired him sooner? Finally, she felt so much remorse after looking into Ruth Hopstef's eyes. How could no one have known she was still being abused? The rumors were all over town, yet no one had done a thing to stop it. Not even Lena Maleno.

Eli had a sixth sense about Lena. "Baby, this isn't your fault."

Lena smiled at him. It was hard to convince her brain of that. "I wish it felt that way."

This was the first time in weeks that she had come home to Eli. She had longed to be here, just the two of them. No chaos, no noise.

"Lena, it's because of who you are."

Lena smiled again. "Eli, will you take a different way home for me?" Eli looked at her, confused. "Just humor me."

She led him to the cottage and looked at him when he pulled up to the drive.

"Come on. I want to show you something."

Eli shrugged and got out of the car. It was unclear why they were here, but he was near her. Nothing else mattered to him. He would take her to every vacant lot in Butler County if she wished.

Lena went up to the porch, took out her key, and opened the door. Eli looked confused again. "You have a key? Lena, what is this place?"

Lena smiled. "It was my grandparents' place. It was left to Galen in their will, but he likes his place in the city. He just wants to stay here occasionally. So? He gave it to me, under the agreement that he can stay here occasionally when he wants to relax. He has the basement bedroom."

Eli just looked at her. "This is ... yours?"

Lena chuckled. "Well, I want it to be ... ours."

Eli looked around as a huge grin appeared on his face. "Ours?" Lena smiled. Eli picked her up and twirled her around. "Bought and paid for?" Lena smiled. "It's ours." Lena nodded again.

Eli went to the kitchen window and looked out. Then, he put his hands up and made a square.

"What are you doing?" Lena asked.

Eli just looked at her. "Oh. Sorry. I was trying to figure out where the barn was going to be."

Lena laughed.

Eli kissed her and hugged her again. "Let's sit on our couch, shall we?" Lena followed him.

Eli suddenly started wringing his hands. "Okay. So, you're sitting there, and I'm ... oh! I must go to the car! I'll be right back."

Lena just smiled. Eli, who had changed into a blue suit coat, was back in a second with two dozen red roses. "Eli! What are you doing! Are these for me?"

"Yes. Well, this was supposed to be done at my place tonight, but isn't it nicer here … at our house?"

Lena was confused. "What? Isn't what?"

Eli got down on one knee while Lena's hands went to the sides of her face in shock. "Oh! Oh my!" She knelt and kissed him deeply.

Eli got up and moved away from her as he got back down on one knee. "Lena! You can't do that! Stop distracting me!"

It was impossible for Lena to feel so much love. She wished she knew what she had done in her life to get this lucky.

"Okay. Now, let me get through this."

Lena went over and sat on his knee. "Lena!"

Lena just kissed his nose. "I promise. I won't touch you at all. Go ahead."

Eli just gave an exasperated sigh. "Okay, fine. Look. You have no idea what you have done to me, Helena Joy Maleno. I can change the world when I'm with you. There is no end to the feeling in my heart. I love you so much it's like … this overwhelming pain when something is wrong. And I instantly want to scoop you up in my arms and make you part of just my world and nobody else's."

Lena put her forehead on his. "Oh, Eli. I love that."

"Hey! No touching!"

Lena giggled.

Eli gave another exasperated sigh. "Oh, I'm screwing this all up. Can you just pick the white rose out of the center of the flowers?"

Lena looked amid the bouquet to find one white rose. She was all caught up in the romance of this whole thing; it remained a complete surprise to her.

When she pulled it out, there was the most beautiful diamond ring she had ever seen, attached.

"Eli! How did you ever ..."

Eli cut her off. "Lena, you are my best friend among everything. Did you hear me? My *best* friend. I never want to be away from you again. Ever. Please say you'll marry me. I'll try so hard to—"

Eli had no opportunity to finish. Lena slipped the ring on her finger as he was proposing, then she kissed him so hard they both fell over.

When she landed on top of him, they were both giggling. Then, Lena put her finger to his lips, so he quieted. Then, Lena said the words Eli had wanted to hear for so long. "Eli Miller, I will not only marry you, but I will also follow you to the ends of the earth if you want."

Eli pulled her to him and kissed her passionately.

Eli carried his fiancée to their new bedroom. As he laid her on the bed, he stopped kissing her. "Lena, we haven't made love since ... I mean ... are you okay?"

Lena sat up on her elbows and touched the side of his face with her hand, stroking his bottom lip. "Eli, I love you. It's time for me to move on with my life. Make love to me, Eli Miller."

He did as he was asked. They showed their love for each other all night long. Eli and Lena shared both laughter and tears that night. But mostly, they shared the one thing they valued most in the world. Love.

CHAPTER *35*

Lena was overjoyed. The next few weeks, her engagement seemed to fly by. She and Eli had officially moved in, so he no longer had to pay rent on his place. Allie was taking them to a surprise getaway, and they were just getting ready to leave. Lena used to love surprises, but lately she was not that fond of them. Not having the heart to disappoint Allie, she relented.

"Allie, I can't get over the change in you this summer!"

Allie just smiled as she suddenly turned down an all-too-familiar road. Lena could feel her chest tighten, so she reached into her purse and put her hand on her inhaler.

"Allie, what's going on …"

They turned up the lane to Derek Hopstef's house.

Allie noticed the instant stress and panic in Lena. She put her hand on Lena's. "Lena, do you trust me?"

Lena knew Allie would never hurt her, but she was still quiet. "Allie, I'm trying to trust again. I really am."

Eli, in the back seat, piped up. "Allie, I don't like this either …"

Allie pulled the car over right before they got to the house. "Look, guys. I promise. Derek is still in jail. If he were anywhere near here, he would go right back there because of the restraining order."

198

Lena mumbled under her breath. "Yeah, right, after he killed one of us."

Allie just looked at her with knowing eyes. "Lena, please. I promise."

Lena decided to protest once more. "Allie, this is his house."

Allie turned on the car and drove the rest of the way. When they arrived, she turned the car off and got out of the car, looking at Lena and Eli. "Well? Are you ready? Let's go!"

Lena and Eli just looked at each other. Allie was awfully happy about this as she rushed ahead of them into the house. Suddenly, Hunter and Rebecca pulled up and exited their SUV.

Although Lena was stressed, she was happy to see Hunter and Rebecca. Lena and Hunter were getting along very well, and he was head over heels in love with Rebecca, who adored him. She was so happy for her friend. She took such good care of Hunter.

"Uh, what's going on?" Hunter was just as confused as they were.

Eli looked at Hunter and shook his head. "Your guess is as good as mine."

At that moment, Dirk came barreling out of the house, all smiles. He put his arms around Allie. Lena found it amusing that his large hands could fit entirely around Allie's teeny waist.

"Oh yay! The final four are here!"

A frustrated Eli was too exasperated to allow this to go on. He needed answers.

"For what!"

Dirk just smiled devilishly. "Come inside! See for yourself."

Eli just groaned. He hated surprises with the fire of a thousand suns. He was about to burst with frustration, and it made Rebecca giggle. Hunter and Rebecca went into the house. Then, Allie turned to Lena and Eli.

Allie looked at Eli. "Are you sure you want to see what's inside?"

Eli was about fifteen different shades of red at this point, which made Allie laugh hysterically. "Okay, okay! Eli, calm down. I just couldn't help myself!"

Lena touched Eli's arm and giggled a little before Eli shot her a look. "Allie, really. Eli is going to explode all over this porch if you don't do something."

Allie giggled again. "Okay. Come in."

They walked in and everyone popped up and yelled, "Surprise!"

Eli jumped, and Lena laughed. There was an engagement cake on the table. Lena went over and took some icing with her finger. She always used to do that when she was a little girl and always got yelled at.

"Lena!" Lois yelled.

Lena looked sheepishly at her mother. "Sorry, Mama. Old habits ..."

Lena looked at everyone. "Oh, this is all so wonderful. Thank you all!" She looked at Eli, who was settling down, but not quite ready to speak yet. "Eli, isn't this wonderful?"

Eli still looked bothered by something.

Dirk started to get worried. "Eli, man, what is it?"

Eli started to pace. "I wish I could enjoy this party. But a Hopstef, especially Derek, could walk in any minute! I mean, didn't you think of that, Dirk?"

Dirk looked like he had swallowed a canary. Then, he said slowly. "No ... they really can't ..."

Eli looked at him like he was insane. "This is the Hopstef ranch, Dirk!"

Dirk went to the desk and pulled out a manila folder. He handed it to Eli, who opened it guardedly. Everyone watched as Eli's eyes protruded from his face and his jaw dropped, causing Dirk to howl with laughter.

"No, this is not the Hopstef ranch. This is the ranch of Dirk and Allison Catan, who were married at city hall last Tuesday."

Everyone stopped what they were doing and turned to Dirk, who was putting his arm around Allie.

Charlie broke the silence. "Wait. You got married? Without us?"

Lois broke through the couple and took Allie by the arm, then frantically pulled her into the middle of the room to scold her. "Allison Hope, how could you!"

Allie was fully prepared for this.

Allie motioned for everyone to sit down. "I want everyone to sit down and hear me out. I love you all. But, big and flashy? That's not me. It's never been me. People looking at me all day in a dress I would never wear on a normal day. Having to say things to Dirk in public that I want to only be between him and me and no one else. That's not who I am, Mama. Please try and understand."

Although everyone was stunned, Lois nodded. Yes, that really did fit Allie. "Can we at least throw a wedding picnic? You can wear what you want."

Dirk interjected. "As long as it's here. On our ranch."

Everyone was apprehensive at first, but after a few minutes, everyone made peace with their decision. It was Dirk and Allie's choice, and they were going to be happy for them.

Allie wanted so much to play hostess and get on with the party. "Now can we please get on with this night that is supposed to be about Eli and Lena?"

Dirk stopped her. "Almost."

Eli turned around with a sour look on his face. He was not having any more surprises tonight.

Dirk walked over to Galen. "I have one more surprise that just drove up. Galen, you can hate me forever, but you need to face this. Everyone is facing fears and moving on. It's time for you to do the same, brother. And I *am* your brother now."

Galen looked suspiciously at him. "What does that mean, exactly?"

Through the door walked the raven-haired beauty from the restaurant. Galen gasped. He was speechless, breathless, and felt like he was having a heart attack. He had never seen her look so beautiful.

"Catherine." Her name came out as a whisper on his tongue. It felt so good to say, and it had been so long since he said her name. His beautiful Catherine.

She just looked at him and returned his salutation. "Hello, Galen."

CHAPTER 36

To Galen, this was inconceivable. He felt weak and thought he was going to faint. He just stared at her, trying to comprehend Catherine's presence.

"Catherine. I ..."

As a good sister should, Allie decided to butt in.

"So, I have homemade ice cream churning in the barn. Galen, would you take Catherine and go check on it for me? It should be getting ready to come to a stop, so you may have to stay with it for a few minutes if that's okay?"

Gale gratefully kissed his sister on the cheek. He knew what she was doing, so he took the hint and led Catherine by the hand and out of the kitchen.

Slowly, they walked to the barn in silence. While they walked, neither one could help but steal a glance at the other. They both still loved one another so much.

Once they were in the barn, Galen began to pace in front of the ice-cream maker, searching for the right words.

It was Catherine who began. She caught Gale's hand while he walked over to her during his pacing and pulled him down on a bench in the barn. "How about I start the conversation? Hello, Galen. My God, you look so incredibly gorgeous right now. I forgot how sexy you really were."

Galen looked at her incredulously. Catherine, always the lady, had never said anything like that to him. Ever.

His response was questioning. "Uh, thank you?"

Catherine sighed. "You're stunned that I would say such a thing." She slowly began to walk around the barn, thinking while she paced.

Galen looked at her as if he were searching for someone else in her eyes. "A little, to be honest."

The ice-cream maker shut off. Galen took it and headed for the door while yelling, "Be right back," over his shoulder.

Catherine continued her slow march around the barn. Galen came in and stole a long glance without her realizing it. Her long, flowing black hair that he was never allowed to touch and her milky tan skin he was never allowed to caress. The lips he'd kissed that always seemed a little cool.

He shook himself out of his daydream. "Uh, I'm back."

Catherine smiled warmly, which was something else Galen never remembered. "Ice cream finished?"

Galen nervously started wringing his hands. "They said they would save us some." Catherine nodded.

Galen leaned against the door. He looked lean and appetizing, although that was not his intention. Catherine imagined taking this opportunity to just take him in her arms. She imagined peeling off every piece of clothing to expose that beautiful body. Sighing, she told herself to pull it together, like she always did. Show no emotion.

"You are probably wondering why I'm here."

Galen laughed nervously. "Yes, I would find an explanation very helpful."

It seemed to Galen that they were two gladiators circling each other. They kept checking each other out to find out how defensive they needed to be while taking quiet moments to think of their next offensive tactic.

Catherine looked down. "I owe you an explanation. When I reconnected with Dirk, I took my chance."

She decided to be brave. That was how she promised herself she would change. This was it. If this was what she wanted, she had to fix what she had destroyed. She had to be direct, and she had to be brave. She moved over to Galen. She was going to be brave, no matter how sexy he looked leaning on that doorframe.

"Galen, I love you. There it is. I. Love. You." She had to blurt it out before she lost her nerve.

Galen had a shocked look on his face. He moved past her out of the doorway and started pacing again. He put his head in his hands while he paced. The words he had needed to hear much sooner than today were so confusing to him now.

Galen whipped around and addressed her. "You *love* me? How in the world am I supposed to believe that? Is this a trick? Is there a camera in this barn?"

Catherine smoothly walked over to him as she exhaled and touched the side of his face. Galen thought he was going to lose his balance. Her touch melted him.

"Galen, I'm allowed to love you now. I have always loved you."

Galen pulled her hand away and whispered to her. "What does that even mean, Catherine? I am so tired of having to figure out riddles in order to be in a relationship."

He moved to a stool and shook his head.

Catherine moved beside him and put her hand on the back of his neck. "I've always loved you. But my father had me in an arranged marriage. He is a powerful man. I am not as strong as Mary Ann. I couldn't defy my father like she did, marrying Dirk. And, in the end? She wasn't as strong as she thought she was."

Galen turned his head to the side and looked at her. "I'm not good enough for your father? A successful lawyer? From a successful family? What does one have to do to be good enough for your father, Catherine?"

Catherine put her hands in her lap. "It has nothing to do with that. He had my marriage arranged since I was a child. When I fell in love with you, I heard about it every day. 'How could you, you stupid girl?' Or 'How could you do this to us?' And my personal favorite, 'God hates me. Girls! Why would he give me girls?'"

Galen could feel his heart sink. All the reasons in the back of his mind were null and void. Catherine had broken his heart because her father had broken hers. "So, your father was emotionally blackmailing you?"

Catherine looked down and sighed. Slowly, she looked up at Galen. She had never looked warm and vulnerable to Galen. Never. "I pushed you away, Galen, because I wanted to protect you. But I eventually cracked."

Galen remembered all of this, and now it was making sense in his head. "And now?"

Catherine stood up and leaned against a pole. "I am estranged from my family. I can't take it anymore, Galen. I haven't talked to them in months. If they can't accept me for who I am and who I want to be, I don't intend to go back."

Galen just looked at her, surprised and hesitant about what to say. Catherine came back to him and knelt in front of him. She was pleading with him now. "Galen, when I saw you at the Crab Shack that day, my heart broke into a million pieces. I made Mary Ann tell me where Dirk was, and I got ahold of him. I forced all this information out of him. Please don't blame him."

Galen got up and started his pacing again. He answered her coldly. "And the rest is history."

When Galen turned around, he noticed that Catherine looked deflated, losing a little hope. Galen admitted that he felt a bit good about that. He wanted her to hurt at least a little bit, but Catherine was persistent.

"I'm stronger now, Galen. I'm here to get back what I love. I won't take no for an answer!" She briskly walked over to Galen, threw her arms around him, and kissed him long, slow, and steady.

Galen was reeling. His brain was telling him not to kiss her back, but his heart was way too strong. The love he had for her came flooding back and he kissed her with all the passion that was left in his soul. An entire flood of emotion coursed through his veins.

They sank onto the barn floor, and Catherine began unbuttoning his shirt.

Galen stopped her. "No, Catherine. Not like this."

Catherine looked at him. "Look me in the eye and tell me you don't love me, Galen Maleno. Tell me you stopped loving me and that you've moved on."

Gale stared at her and a smile slyly worked its way across his face. Catherine had won.

"I thought so. Please tell me, Galen."

Galen got up and rebuttoned his shirt. "I love you, Catherine. It's always been you. But you've always known that, haven't you?"

Catherine got up and went to him. "What does that mean?"

Galen looked at her. "There is nothing I want more than to make love to you right now, trust me. But I won't. You hurt me. You don't get to just tell me that you love me and then make love to me and take over my heart again, Catherine. I love you. But you will have to work your way back into my heart again. That's fair."

Catherine paused for a moment, then kissed his cheek. "I accept the challenge, Galen. I will prove to you that this time is different. I will not break your heart again."

Galen put his hand on her cheek. "If you do, don't ever come back." He gently pulled his hand away, turned, and walked out of the barn.

Catherine knew he was serious. This was her last and only chance to make it up to Galen. There would be no third chance.

Chapter 37

Running out of the barn, Catherine caught up to him, pulled Galen by the hand, and kissed him passionately one more time. "What was that for?" Galen smiled.

"I don't want you to forget that I love you. I will keep saying it and showing it. Don't forget it." Catherine was different, and Galen just had to decide whether to believe it.

Dirk walked in on another fiery kiss. "Well! All is well here?"

Galen produced a big smile on this face and shot Catherine a look.

Dirk just grunted. "Okay, how about we never discuss what may or may not have just happened in my new barn? Come on. Let's go tell everyone what an awesome matchmaker I am." Galen was about to protest, then he decided against it.

Entering the house, it was Dirk that stopped in his tracks. "What are you doing here?"

Dirk had not signed up for the two-for-one deal, but there she was. Catherine was accompanied by her very pregnant sister, Mary Ann. The woman who had torn Dirk's heart out with a spoon. She had been waiting in the car, mustering up the courage to face Dirk.

"She came with me, Dirk. I'm sorry. I didn't realize you were happily married."

Mary Ann's jaw dropped. "Wait. Married? *You are married?*"

Allie, in all her strength and wisdom, walked right up to Mary Ann. "Hello. I'm Allison. Allison Catan."

With that, Mary Ann ran out the door. Catherine just sighed. Mary Ann was always dramatic and immature. "I guess we are leaving now. Again, I'm so sorry. Galen, I'll see you later." She kissed him softly and sweetly in front of his family. Galen had never had a kiss feel so blissful.

Suddenly, something came to his mind, causing him to run to the door. "Uh, Catherine?"

Catherine turned to Galen. "Yes?"

Galen gave her a knowing look. "You have some explaining to do tomorrow, dear."

Catherine looked at him, confused.

"Excuse me?" Catherine was unclear about what explanation he was referring.

Galen knew he had caught her in a lie. "You haven't spoken to your family in months? Remember that?"

Catherine looked at him with wide eyes. "I didn't think that applied to my sister!"

Galen began to turn around. "You only get one chance to explain tomorrow, Catherine. Choose your words carefully."

Catherine nodded solemnly as she entered the car, suddenly realizing that it was going to be a lot harder to get Galen back than she thought.

CHAPTER 38

Lena was still getting her bearings at work. To her surprise, it was William that had been helping her with trail rides. She had taken a liking to Maribel, who was a solid horse with a cute personality.

Charlie had slowly started to enjoy trail riding. Gracie still had absolutely zero interest, but it was nice to see Charlie and Lois coming in from this ride.

"Mama, I think I'm ready to go out tomorrow."

Lois looked shocked yet proud. "Well, that's good, dear. I could use a break, and Charlie here was just telling me how much she was looking forward to it."

The look on Charlie's face was shocked. Lena had been played, but she paid no mind. She knew her mom was just making her feel better.

Charlie was reluctant. "Yeah ... sounds like fun, Lena!"

Charlie plastered on a smile, making Lena smile to herself. Charlie had been trying so hard to behave lately.

"I think Charlie may be able to lead this one!" Lois exclaimed as she was dismounting her horse.

Charlie suddenly looked horrified. It was quite different to see Charlie unsure of herself for once.

"What? Mama, I'm not ready for that!"

Lena took a page from her mother's book. "Sure, you are, Charlie! I'll be right there in case something goes wrong. You can do this."

Charlie looked thoughtful. "What am I going to wear?"

Lena smiled to herself. Some things never changed.

Charlie immediately brushed her horse and went off to the barn to plan her outfit.

Lois came up to Lena. "You are sure about this, dear?"

"Mama. It has been months. You all need to quit treating me like I'm made of glass."

Lois nodded her head in approval. It was so hard for her to let Lena go. It was so hard to watch Lena go through such unsurmountable pain. It was hard allowing herself to believe that she was okay. "Okay, but if you need anything ..."

Lena went over and hugged her mother. "I love you, Mama. I mean that."

"And I love you, Helena Joy." Lois and Lena hugged each other until Lena released.

"I'm going to see Galen at work."

Bidding her mother farewell, she turned to look for Eli, who was shoeing Princess.

"Ready for lunch?"

Eli came over and kissed her tenderly. "Always for you. What did you have in mind?"

His seductive look told her the plans each one had in mind were different from the other. After he kissed her neck, Lena playfully pushed him away. "Eli! Not *that*!"

Eli frowned. "Bummer. Rain check."

Then he winked at her. He was obviously in a good mood!

"Going to the city to have lunch with Galen."

Eli took off his apron. "Sounds good! Let's go!"

Lena texted Galen and told him the plan. He chose an adorable little sandwich shop downtown. They ordered, and Lena got right to the point.

"Galen, you know the deal. Have the famous talk with Eli. I want to get to the bottom of this Catherine thing."

Both men looked shocked.

Eli was the first to blurt out. "What?"

Gale looked slightly amused. "Lena ..."

"Come on! Get it over with!"

Galen busted into laughter. "Lena, you are something else."

Eli was becoming frustrated. "Oh no. You guys know how much I hate being left out of stuff!"

Galen explained the pact they had made, then both men started laughing, while Lena began to feel heated.

"So ... until you play big brother about our relationship, you don't have to tell her about Catherine?"

Galen looked proud of himself. "That's right."

More laughter.

Lena was becoming infuriated now. "Hey! I'm not joking!"

Galen and Eli settled down. Eli put his hands under his chin to keep from laughing, and Galen put on his lawyer face.

"Okay, here goes. Eli, I can't think of a more honest, more devoted man for my sister. I'm so glad she found you. But. I must warn you. If you ever hurt her for any reason, I will ..."

Lena was exasperated. "Well?"

Galen glanced down at her, toying with her temper. "Lena, give me a second! I'm trying to remember what I said I would do."

Lena was livid now. "Break both his legs in six places! Now, come on!"

Eli was desperately trying not to laugh at this situation. Galen was having way too much fun. "Oh yeah. Thanks, Lena! Let me start over."

Lena was exasperated, and the men could see a fury ignite in her eyes. Galen thought it best to stop toying with her, even though laughter would not stop releasing from the pressure valve in his mouth, no matter how hard he tried.

"Eli. If you hurt my sister, I get to break both your legs in six places."

Eli snorted, which caused Galen to release a wild fit of laughter, causing Lena to punch them both in the arm. "Ow!" Galen pretended to look hurt for a moment, then began to snicker again.

This time, it was Eli who was messing with Lena's fiery temper. "Galen, is that six places in each leg, or six altogether?"

Galen pretended to look thoughtful for a moment. "I'll have to get back to you on that."

"Oh, please do."

Suddenly, they both looked at Lena, who looked like she was going to start a tirade. Both men instantly settled down, and Eli took on a serious nature.

Eli ran his fingers through a few strands of Lena's hair and smiled at her, bringing her back to reality. "I'm sorry, baby. I love Lena with all my heart, Galen. I would rather die than hurt her. She is my entire world. If I hurt her, I would lie down and allow you to break all of my limbs as many times as you want."

Both men looked at Lena as if to say "satisfied?"

"So, that's it." Lena rolled her eyes. "*That's* the big scary brother talk?" Gale just shrugged. Lena rolled her eyes again. "Okay, Gale. You know the deal. What's up with this Catherine?"

Galen sighed, knowing he could avoid this no longer.

"Years ago, Catherine and I met at a horse auction. I was looking for racehorses, she was looking for breeding stallions. We spent the whole weekend together, and I fell in love with her instantly. Things were so easy and free with her. It was the best weekend of my life. We spent time together when we got back, and everything was good. Until I met her father. Alexander Freeman."

A look of shock hit Eli and Lena.

"*The* Alexander Freeman?"

"The Alexander Freeman who breeds Triple-Crown horses?" Eli knew of him well.

"Yes, her name is Catherine Freeman. Dirk was married to Mary Ann Freeman. Mr. Freeman decided he didn't like me. I wasn't grounded enough. I was too wild."

Lena just looked at him in shock. "You have got to be kidding."

Galen grinned. "Think back, Lena. I was not always like this. Look at your timeline. When did I change?"

Lena caught on. Galen had settled down for Catherine.

"I soon discovered that Catherine and Mary Ann are completely controlled by their father. Brainwashed. To be with her meant I had to be controlled by him too. And I was going to do it! I loved her that much."

Lena looked at Galen with sad eyes. This sounded nothing like the confident lawyer brother she knew. Galen's life as a horse breeder would be fleeting, as he would never be happy.

"She froze me out instead. One day, my belongings were on our porch with a Dear John note. I never saw her again until that day at the restaurant and your party."

"And now he's figuring out if it's worth it to throw his heart into the ring again." Lena looked up to see Catherine standing behind her.

At that moment, Lena decided she was distrustful of stalker ex-girlfriends.

"How did you find me?" Galen was taken off guard, which was not his favorite place to be.

"You weren't at the office. You were either here, at Young Chang's, or Parker's Pizza."

Galen was a little honored that she remembered and also a little freaked out.

Catherine put her hand out for Lena to shake and gave her a warm smile. "Hi. I'm Catherine Freeman. I don't believe we have been properly introduced."

Lena reluctantly shook her hand. "Helena Maleno. Big sister."

"Eli Miller. Future brother-in-law."

A light bulb went off in Catherine's head. "Oh! Congratulations! I'm so sorry to crash your party."

Lena decided to keep it cool yet friendly. "Quite all right."

There was a moment of awkward silence.

Catherine knew she was out of time before Galen had to return to work. "I don't suppose you would be kind enough to give me a few moments alone with Galen. I'm so sorry to interrupt your lunch. I won't be in the city long today."

Lena suddenly got territorial. "Well, actually …"

Eli quickly interrupted. "Not at all. We must be getting back. You have a trail ride, Lena?"

Lena pouted. "Yes, I do."

Eli got up and shook Catherine's hand. He gave Lena a look that told her to do the same. Lena did and replied with, "It was lovely to meet you!" The goodbye was much peppier than Lena meant it.

"Okay, let's get going." Lena kissed Galen, and Eli pulled her out of the restaurant before she started any more shenanigans.

Galen smiled. Catherine better watch her step. Lena was tough.

"Likewise!" Catherine tried to shout after Lena, but Eli had already whisked her away before she said something she would regret.

Lena turned around and gave Catherine Freeman her best "I've got your number, watch your step, lady" stare. Eli realized it was going to be an awfully long ride home.

CHAPTER 39

"Who does she think she is? Galen can't be serious about this." Lena was fuming, and Eli tried not to laugh. He loved her fire and fury.

It took Lena all of twenty seconds to ignite into a rage of fire about Galen and Catherine. She was rambling nonstop, her hands waving furiously, and Eli thought she was going to hit herself in the face. She kept turning to the side in the passenger seat and asking for his input. He just smiled and allowed her to ask for his opinion, giving him not a second to chime in. This went on for about ten minutes.

Eli decided he should probably try to calm her down before she developed a heart condition. "Honey ... Lena ... Do you want my honest opinion or not?"

Lena looked daggers at him. "Well, haven't I been asking for it all this time?" Lena was annoyed now, especially since Eli had been smiling during her entire fit of rage.

"Well then, pipe down so I can give it to you! I haven't been able to fit a comment into this entire full-blown conversation for about fifteen minutes."

Lena slumped back in the seat with her arms crossed in front of her, pouting, knowing what Eli was going to say. When it came to Galen, her only brother, Lena was territorial and protective.

"Lena, there is absolutely nothing you can do about this. And there is nothing you should do about this. Galen is a grown man. You have to let him work this out."

Eli counted back in his head … *five … four … three … three … two …* "But, Eli!" There it was.

Eli shook his head. Lena slumped back in the seat in the same position again, knowing he was right.

"Honey. Can you trust me on this? I know it hurts that you are no longer the central woman in Galen's life."

Lena came out of the seat and opened her mouth as if she were going to say something, but Eli stopped her. "You are the center of my universe now. Can that be enough for you?"

Lena's resented that Eli knew exactly how to melt all those walls away every time.

"Fine. But if she hurts him again …"

Eli thought he better not press his luck. "Then I promise you can yell at her all you want, and I won't stand in your way. Not until then, Lena."

This time she just sat back in the seat and put her hands in her lap. Her blood was no longer boiling now, and she felt calmer. Eli decided to give her a few minutes to continue to sort all of this out in her head, then he would attempt to change the subject.

"So, I hear you're going back out on a trail ride tomorrow. I'm proud of you."

Lena was grateful for the change of subject. "Yes. I'm ready, Eli. I'm tired of just brushing horses all day."

Eli felt she was ready, as well. She was not full strength yet and could still cry at the craziest times. Her emotions were still a bit heightened and raw, but she had made so much progress. Eli felt that getting back into the things she loved to do was the best way for her to move forward.

As they pulled up the driveway, they saw a woman running from the barn, causing Eli to pull over.

They both got out of the car. The woman came closer and eventually they were able to identify her.

"Rebecca, are you okay?" Eli was always a gentleman to every woman he encountered.

Rebecca was even more drop-dead gorgeous when she cried. Usually, Lena hated those women who were beautiful even when they cried, but she adored Rebecca so much, she overlooked it.

"I honestly can't take it anymore!"

Rebecca was only half crying, more of an angry cry than anything. Lena had never seen Rebecca like this! She was usually so easygoing and carefree. This angry side of Rebecca was a conundrum to Lena, and it worried her.

Suddenly, Hunter came out of the barn and began walking toward Rebecca.

"Rebecca! Rebecca!" He picked up his pace when he realized she'd stopped closer to the barn.

Eli and Lena leaned against the truck inconspicuously. Rebecca just stood there, obviously contemplating her next move. Lena decided to play dumb. "What's going on, Hunter?"

Hunter just ignored that Lena was there and completely focused on Rebecca. "Rebecca. He is my dad. What do you expect?"

Rebecca turned toward him and stomped her foot. "He is a *jackass!*"

Eli and Lena turned toward each other. Lena mouthed the words "uh-oh" to Eli. He nodded in agreement while she put her arm around Rebecca in a consoling and supportive manner.

William decided to make matters worse by joining the conversation. Lena and Eli had reached that awkward moment where they were skeptical about whether to leave or stay. They were the ones who knew William best, and they both knew that William had a temper. Rebecca and Hunter's relationship was new, and no one knew Rebecca more than Lena. They decided to stay.

William opened his mouth, and as usual, he just made things ten times worse. "Lookie here, girlie. I meant what I said. You are a distraction to Hunter's success! You don't know anything about horses."

An upset Rebecca just screamed to herself, stomped her foot, and turned away from him. Lena gasped in shock as she attempted to console her, but Rebecca shrugged her away. Hunter lifted his head up, looking to God for direction, and Eli closed his eyes, trying to come up with the right words to say. Under his breath, so only Lena could hear, Eli asked himself how William had ever been able to woo one woman enough to produce a child, let alone two. Lena giggled, prompting Rebecca to turn around and give her a disparaging look. Lena returned to her and hugged her supportively.

Eli grabbed William by the arm and yanked him away from the group a few steps. He started to whisper harshly at him. "William, what are you doing?"

William was indignant. "Just stating the truth, like I always do!"

Eli's hand hit his forehead. He then looked at William. "Well, stop it!"

While Eli was talking to William, Lena decided to talk to Hunter, leaving Rebecca alone with her own thoughts. "Why aren't you defending her? This is supposed to be your girlfriend!"

Hunter started to pace and nervously run his hands through his hair, which made Lena wonder if all men did this when they were discouraged.

Obviously hearing the conversation, Rebecca turned to hear Hunter's answer. He looked as if he was going to respond, but just sighed and dropped his head, causing an exasperated Rebecca to storm off.

Hunter stopped pacing and yelled after her. "Rebecca, please stop. Rebecca, I'm sorry! He's my *dad*!"

Lena sighed. "Let her go. I've got her."

Eli put his arm out in front of Lena. "Oh, no, you don't."

Lena glared at him. "Excuse me?"

Eli stood his ground as he was the only one that could when it came to vivacious Lena. "Let her go, Lena. You are too emotionally connected. Let Rebecca settle down. You need to let people handle their own problems. You aren't meant to fix things all the time."

Lena just looked at Eli, who was preparing to get a tongue lashing, but to his surprise, it never came. Instead, Lena just told him how she felt, which surprised him. "Eli, she's my friend. It's my fault that she even got involved with these two lunkheads."

Eli giggled at her term of endearment, then sighed in frustration as he waved her on, and Lena was off, chasing after Rebecca.

She found Rebecca in the driver's seat of her car, crying uncontrollably. Lena knocked on the window as the door was locked. "Rebecca, honey, please let me in." Rebecca could barely find the unlock button. When she did, Lena carefully opened the door and slowly sat in the passenger seat. She hugged Rebecca for a few minutes.

"I'm okay. Really. I just needed a good cry."

"You sure?"

"Yes. I just don't get it! Why won't he stand up to him?"

Rebecca looked at Lena with those big beautiful eyes of hers. Lena found a napkin in the tissue box and handed it to her.

"He likes having a dad, Rebecca. He's afraid to go back to not having a dad again. From what I understand, his mother is no picnic."

Deep down, Rebecca knew that William was Hunter's biggest weakness. William had given up Lena once. He would not do it again.

In the most hushed whisper, Rebecca looked at Lena and asked the most painful question. "Lena, why did I have to fall in love with him?"

Not knowing Rebecca was in love with him, Lena tried not to look shocked. As wishy-washy a place as Hunter was in emotionally, Lena thought that was dangerous.

"Does he love you?" Lena asked, trying to assess the depths of their relationship.

Rebecca looked down. "Yes. He was the first one to say it." Rebecca smiled and blushed. Lena had not realized their relationship had advanced at warp speed.

"We have a great relationship! Until William comes around. Then it's all about 'Race season is next month' and 'Can't be distracted.' Rebecca had a sarcastic tone and used air quotes, which made Lena snicker to herself. She liked saucy Rebecca.

After a moment of silence, Lena sighed, knowing what she had to do. She knew that someone had to try to reason with William. Eli had tried and failed, and Hunter had too much at stake. It had to be her. Quietly, she brought the idea up to Rebecca. "I could talk to William for you."

Rebecca turned in her seat and looked hopeful. "Oh, would you, Lena?"

Lena, looking less than enthused, answered her. "Yes, of course. I would do anything for you, Rebecca." She gave her a half-hearted smile, followed by a hug, and exited the car.

Before she closed the door, Lena said, "Now, go back and get Hunter. I'll talk to William."

Rebecca was already looking down the road, squinting. Then, she immediately smiled. "I don't think I have to." She was pointing as she reached for the door handle.

Lena looked up the drive and saw Hunter walking down the road. Rebecca flew out of the car and into Hunter's arms. Lena understood now. They loved each other more than she realized.

Lena headed back up to the barn where Eli and William were already in a heated argument.

"You can't expect him to work night and day! *You* don't work night and day!" Eli's eyes flared, and Lena thought he looked incredibly sexy.

"Stay out of this, Eli!" Tempers were starting to flare. Lena knew that tone and decided she better put a stop to this before Eli's emotions kicked in. He was still suffering from the tragedies he had suffered the past few months.

"Okay, okay. You've ruined enough lives. Knock it off, William." Lena stopped herself, not meaning to sound cruel. That sounded much better in her head.

William decided to answer her just as cruelly. "Aw. Look who suddenly wants to become a family."

Lena was starting to flare now. Eli was about to say something, but Lena put up her hand. He knew that she had to get out what she was going to say. There was no stopping this.

"I gave *Hunter* that horse. Not you. If he wants to spend time with Rebecca, then that's what he is going to do. You need to come out of this ivory tower you think you somehow deserve, or you will be living there forever, party of one. Hunter and Rebecca can still have a relationship and have a racehorse. Just because you didn't want to have a relationship your entire life doesn't mean other people don't want it."

William just stood there, shocked. His voice was low, and his brow was furrowed. He was cool when he answered. "He's the only one that gives me a chance. He treats me like a dad."

Lena turned around. Although that stung, she was unfaltering. "That doesn't mean you get to monopolize his time. You don't get to control him selfishly. You can't make up for lost time, William. It's too late. You can only move forward."

The look on William's face showed Lena she had made him think. He slowly sat down, coming to this revelation in his mind.

William's epiphany came out of him slowly and calmly. "I have been doing that, haven't I? I have been torturing that poor girl because I am afraid to lose Hunter. What is wrong with me?"

Lena suddenly felt bad for William. She went and sat beside him, searching for the right words.

"I haven't been really helpful. I've been really hard on you concerning our past and haven't been really forgiving. I'm really sorry."

William looked up at her, surprised. Lena looked pensive. She got up and instantly changed to a cheerier tone. "Besides. You realized what you did wrong. You can fix it now!"

William stood up now. "How?"

Lena took William's hands in hers. "Just talk to them. Change. And, although I know this is hard for you … apologize.

William sighed. "My three worst qualities."

Lena looked at Eli and smiled.

"If Hunter genuinely loves you like I know he does, he will understand. If Rebecca loves Hunter like I know she does, she will understand. She's a really good person, William."

William looked at Lena. "And … you?"

Lena looked down, then her eyes slowly looked up at him. "William, I have always loved you. It's hard for me to see you with different eyes, but I'm learning. I never stopped loving you, though. You've been here forever, and you've always looked out for all of us. You're obstinate, bullheaded, mouthy, rude sometimes, and downright mean at others. But we all know your heart. Whether you like it or not, you have an amazingly large heart. And we all love you for it. I don't know if I can ever call you Dad. But please know that I love you as William, just as I always have. Is that enough for you?"

William hugged Lena and said, "You might be the smartest person I know."

Eli smiled. "Well? I know where you get your bullheadedness from."

Lena grinned. "Really? Which one is more bullheaded? Lois or William?"

Eli thought for a minute. "Okay, it's a draw. You really had no hope." Lena smacked him playfully. Eli kissed her. "Let's go home."

Lena liked the sound of that.

CHAPTER *40*

Lena woke up later that week, feeling reenergized. Charlie's trail ride had gone famously. Although Gracie took no interest in the horses, everyone was shocked to find that her accounting skills were sensational, and Lena was grateful. It was the part of the business she hated most, and Gracie was a mastermind. Lena was awestruck at the way Gracie just figured numbers in her head as if it were a language she spoke fluently.

The twins were ready with her shoes and coat as she came downstairs.

Lena looked at them curiously. "What's this?"

Rebecca and Allie came through the door then, followed by Lois. Allie squealed, "Are we ready?"

Lena now had a suspicious look on her face. Allie loved surprises. Lena? Not so much.

It was Gracie that squealed next. "Bridal dress shopping kidnapping!"

Lena started to laugh. "Gracie, you can't kidnap someone who's willing to go!"

Now Charlie squealed. Lena winced at the amount of squealing in a short span of time. "Oh, but there's more! This Saturday is another bridal event! Are you excited?"

Lena scrunched up her nose. "What does that even mean?"

Charlie erupted with excitement. "Allie's reception!"

The twins started to clap, and Lena giggled. It was hard not to get caught up in their excitement. She was so glad she had matured enough to know her sisters.

Gracie quieted everyone down. "I'm so excited I could faint. We are going to be spending an obscene amount of money today on my favorite thing. Clothes! And it's going to be on my favorite people. Sisters!"

Lena never thought she would adore the twins so much, but she had grown to love them. This once terribly broken family had come together so beautifully. She wished Daddy had been alive to see it.

Allie stopped everyone before they got too out of hand. "Wait! Hold on just a minute. I never agreed to any reception." The twins just ignored her and continued their planning. Allie tried again. "I'm serious! I said a picnic. I never agreed to a reception!"

Poor Allie. As usual, she had no say in the matter.

Lois just patted her on the shoulder like she did when they were children. It was the "Oh, Allie, just do it. Everyone will love it" pat on the shoulder that Allie despised. Then, Lois continued, her focus elsewhere. "We are waiting on one more."

Charlotte spoke up. "Aw, Mama, come on."

Lena had presumed it was Catherine after Charlotte's whining. She and Galen had made amends and had spent every waking minute together. No one liked her, but everyone was trying. Lois was not one to put up with the twins' whining.

"Charlotte Faith. You stop that right there! You give her a chance for Galen's sake. Let me remind you that this little sisterfest you've all created was not too much not so awfully long ago."

All the sisters, including Lena, just looked down like they did when they were little and were being scolded.

Gracie decided to add to the misery. "She's late."

Just then, Lois' phone buzzed. "Yes, she is. She's pulling up now, and I will hear no fuss from you either, Grazieanna."

Gracie stomped her foot. Grace was the only sister that despised her name. Her official name was Gracie Anna and she was named after her maternal grandmother, Grazieanna Bianchi. She knew Lois meant business when her full name came from her mother's lips with an Italian accent. Gracie was instantly quiet. She was not about to hear it again.

Catherine entered the house to find the Maleno women looking at her, obviously waiting for an explanation. You did not mess with the twins and shopping!

"Whoa. Uh. Sorry. You guys are very punctual people, aren't you?"

It was Rebecca, the outsider, who felt badly for her.

"Come on, Catherine. I'm Hunter's fiancée. You can ride with me and Lena."

Everyone froze. Charlie squealed again. Lena, in her head, wanted to say, "Can everyone just stop squealing?"

"Whoa. Hold the phone!"

Then, Gracie finished her sentence. Lena hated it when they did that. "Did you just say—"

But Gracie stuttered instead of finishing her sentence, so Allie jumped in. "Fiancée?"

Rebecca's hands went up to her mouth as if she were trying hard not to grin. Lena blurted out her remark as she was pulling Rebecca in for a hug. "When were you going to tell us this?"

Rebecca just beamed and held out her hand to a very sparkly square-cut diamond ring with smaller diamonds all around. Everyone except Catherine gushed over it. Much to Lena's dismay, there was more squealing.

Then, Charlotte started jumping up and down. "Whoa. Guys. This is. Triple. Bride. Dress. Shopping! Mama. Have I died? This is heaven, right? I'm actually in heaven?"

Allie stomped her foot. "You are not! I'm not getting a big fancy gown, Charlie!"

Charlotte just waved Allie off. "Oh I know, Allie. But it's your reception. You'll have to wear something. So, technically, it's still your wedding dress. It qualifies!"

Allie just rolled her eyes. There was no winning this argument, so she just started heading for the car with everyone else and got in.

Catherine felt like the third wheel. There was no end to the discomfort and awkwardness she felt, but she was determined to power through. She was strong, and she loved Galen. She was doing this for him. It was only a few hours, right?

Lena looked over at Rebecca. "Why didn't you tell me?" She was obviously a little hurt by this revelation.

Rebecca just smiled. "Lena, this is your day. I don't want to be the center of attention on your day!"

"Rebecca, I don't care about that. I can't believe you wouldn't know that! I'm so happy. We will be sisters!"

Catherine decided she better take her opportunity to cut in now. Not wanting to be a third wheel, she wanted to show her enthusiasm. Rebecca seemed like her best bet, and Lena seemed to be on her best behavior when Rebecca was around. If she could get Lena convinced that she was good for Galen, the others could follow. "How would you feel if I were your sister someday?"

There was dead silence in the car for a few seconds. Suddenly, Lena spoke. "Did Galen pop the question?"

Catherine looked at her naked finger. She would do anything for Galen to pop the question. "No. Hypothetically, of course."

Lena thought for a moment, indecisive about her answer. She had learned from her experience with the twins that she needed to give people a chance. However, Catherine had hurt Galen. She would give Catherine a chance, but she would do so cautiously.

"You've hurt my brother once already."

Catherine instantly went on the defensive. "And you are all making me pay for that. How did Charlie get out of having to pay for hurting your fiancé, Lena?"

Lena looked out the window, not expecting Catherine to know such information. Galen had told her everything. They were obviously remarkably close.

"How did Hunter find himself forgiven for trying to hurt everyone in your family?"

Another morsel of unexpected yet truthful information.

Lena pulled over. Slowly, she turned to Catherine from the driver's seat. "You're right."

Catherine was caught by surprise, not expecting Lena to relent so easily.

"I have an exceedingly long history of being a fighter. I am not great with giving people the benefit of the doubt." Lena looked at Rebecca, who was smiling. Then, she continued. "I'm willing to try harder if you are."

Catherine rushed to answer. "Deal!" She smiled brightly. Then, she looked at Lena and said, "Now, those twin sisters of yours …"

Lena chuckled. "You are on your own! I've known them my whole life and have only gotten along with them for about a year.

They are a piece of work. After a while, loveable pieces of work. But I will be the first to admit that they are an acquired taste."

Rebecca nudged Lena. "We better get going. If we hold up the twins anymore, they might hyperventilate."

Everyone in the car laughed.

Lena looked at her new soon-to-be sister-in-law. "Oh, Rebecca. You have this family figured out already!"

When they got to the dress shop, the twins were in full bridal attire.

Lena looked at them and laughed. "Hey! Who's getting married here?"

Gracie looked annoyed. "Well, Lena. Since you vanished when I explained the plan, I will go over it again. We are all choosing one dress to try on, then it will be easier to bring down your choices. We will go bride by bride."

Lena looked at her suspiciously. "Uh-huh. Gracie, you don't even know what I like."

Charlotte looked at her thoughtfully. "Don't we?"

Lena had to admit. The two dresses they had on were exactly what she would have chosen for herself. Simple, elegant, lacy, and showed off her figure.

Gracie called out for Lois in a sing-song tone. "MAMA!"

Out came Lois in a bridal gown, too. "Girls, this is ridiculous."

Charlotte started to pout. "Mama, you have to join in the fun."

Lois rolled her eyes. Rebecca smiled at Lois. "I will only do this under one condition."

Everyone stopped and awaited Rebecca's response. "Yes. Gracie and Charlotte, we all get to try on a dress that we think the two of you would choose!"

The twins looked at each other. Charlotte squealed yet again. "Oh! A twist in the game! You are going to be the best sister ever."

Lena then spoke up. "I'm only doing this under one condition." Allie rolled her eyes. This could not have been more painful for her if she tried. The twins were mesmerized, and Lena thought their heads would explode.

Gracie could no longer wait out the silence. "*Another* twist?"

"Yes. We play the game, trying to guess what kind of dress Catherine would choose. And she gets to try on dresses as well."

Lois had a suspicious look on her face. She knew Lena, and this was either goodwill or some mastermind plan she was executing.

Everyone fell silent. Slowly, each woman looked over at Catherine, who was suddenly awkwardly aware of herself.

Gracie just exploded. "Are you kidding? More gowns to try on! I wonder if any of the strangers will play with us?"

Everyone broke into laughter. The only ones that looked horrified were the bridal consultants.

After trying what seemed like every gown in the store, Lena chose a simple gown with a lace overlay for her bridal gown and a yellow sundress to wear to Allie's reception on Saturday. Allie chose a light pink sheath dress with chiffon sleeves to wear on Saturday. Rebecca chose a mermaid-style gown with plenty of tulle for her bridal gown. She chose a royal blue A-line dress for Allie's reception. Charlie chose a form-fitting red dress for Saturday, informing everyone in the store that red was her signature color.

Lena thought Gracie looked the most stunning in her wine-colored satin dress that showed off her legs. Everyone held their breath as Lois walked out. She chose a champagne, floor-length chiffon gown. She looked stunning.

"Is something wrong?" Lois asked.

Lena walked up to her and put her hands on her shoulders. "Mama. You are breathtaking!"

"I'm glad you think so. This is what I picked out for your wedding, Lena. Now, if you will excuse me."

She returned moments later. Lena never realized what exquisite taste her mother had. This time she had on a cream-colored suit with a pink satin scarf.

It was Allie that was choked up this time. "Mama. You seriously need to open your own dress shop!"

Lois laughed. "I wouldn't enjoy shopping if it were my job! Now, ladies. We have one more lady to see."

Catherine stepped out in a long navy-blue maxi dress that showed off her complexion. She looked beautiful.

Lena chuckled. "It's a shame we are all getting married. We are beautiful women!"

Charlotte remarked. "Hey. Some of us are still searching. Rebecca? Catherine? Tell us you have brothers!" Rebecca and Catherine both made pouty faces at the twins. "Darn. Well? I tried."

Everyone laughed at Charlie's remark. The ladies were having so much fun.

They all agreed to another shopping trip for dresses for Rebecca's wedding.

Lena's heart was full, even though she had lost so much.

Chapter *41*

Allie looked gorgeous, as did everyone else. Rebecca and Hunter looked like they were in engagement bliss. The twins were talking to two of Dirk's cowboy friends, who were hanging on their every word. Lois and William were getting along famously these days.

Eli came up behind Lena, wrapping his arms around her waist. She could feel his head around hers, and his voice whisper in her ear. "You look stunning. The man you love is a lucky man."

Lena giggled. Then she looked to the side and said, "No, I'm the lucky one." She lifted her chin up so that Eli could kiss her. She was blissfully happy.

When she pulled her head back down, Eli noticed something odd. He turned Lena around. "Lena, you look kind of pale today. Are you sure you're feeling well?"

Lena just put her hand on the side of his face. "Honey. It's so hot here today. I'm just warm."

She was correct. Even for Pennsylvania in June, the weather was unbelievably hot. They had tossed around the idea of moving the reception to the barn. Eli felt her head, then looked at her with concern.

Lena just repeated her answer. "I think I'm just ... just ..." Lena started to feel short of breath. "Oh ... No ... not ... now ..." She could feel herself start to wheeze.

"Lena?" Eli started to panic. She had yet to teach him what to do when she had an asthma attack. Number one on the list was *do not panic*. Keep her calm.

"Purse." The word came out as a wheeze. She was in a full-blown asthma attack.

Eli frantically rooted through her purse for her inhaler. The look in his eyes was painful when it was nowhere to be found. He was much too stressed. The closest person to him was Rebecca.

Eli began to yell. "*Rebecca! Help!*" There was no calming him. He was in full-blown panic mode.

Rebecca rushed over and snapped into action.

"Okay." Rebecca's voice was gentle and calm. "Okay, Lena. First thing. Hold up one finger for yes to my questions, okay? I don't want you to try to use your airway in order to speak, understand?" Lena held up a finger. "Hey, that's great! Good girl."

Rebecca smiled. Eli was still panicking. Rebecca needed to give him something to do. "Okay. Eli, I need you to go to the car and see if she has an inhaler in the glove box, okay? Can you do that?" Eli ran, buying Rebecca some time. "Okay. Lena, can you hear me?" Lena held up a finger. She was still wheezing.

"Okay. Lena, Eli's going to look for an inhaler. In the meantime, I need you to sit up with me. That's perfect. Okay. You and I, we are going to take some long, deep breaths. We are going to try to slow our breaths down just a little bit."

Eli ran back in with an emergency inhaler. "I found it! I found it!"

Rebecca smiled. "Eli, that's good. Now, please call 911."

Eli just looked at her. "I can get her there faster."

Rebecca just looked at him. "Yes, I know. But there will be oxygen in the ambulance for the ride, and that's what she needs. Please call."

Eli nodded frantically and took out his phone. Not thinking straight, he blurted out, "What's the number for 911?"

Lena took her inhaler and was slowly starting to feel better, although she was still struggling.

Hunter had come to Rebecca's side by this point. "I called 911 about five minutes ago, Rebecca. The ambulance is on its way."

Rebecca smiled again. "Thank you, Hunter. Could you stay with Eli, please?" Hunter smiled and nodded.

"Okay, Lena? Remember … you are worked up because you can't breathe. Please try your best to stay calm."

Lena nodded. Rebecca looked at her watch. "Okay. It's been a minute. Go ahead and take your inhaler again." Lena did so. This time the medicine from the inhaler seemed to go in better.

"Lena, that was really great. Now, just stay calm with me, okay?" Lena lifted her finger.

Hunter bent down near Rebecca. "Hey, Eli and I are going to take off for the hospital ahead of you, is that okay?"

Rebecca looked at Hunter, relieved. "That is perfect."

Right after they left, the ambulance came up the drive. Everyone had noticed what was going on by now.

Galen stepped in like he was so used to doing.

"Asthma attack, folks. Nothing to see here. Once she gets oxygen, she will be fine. Happens often. I promise. Please return to Allie and Dirk!" Lena looked at him gratefully.

Allie rushed over as did the twins. Galen stopped her. "Allison, she is fine. This isn't her first time with this affliction.

She will be back soon. Go enjoy your party. She's gonna be madder than a bull if you don't, and you know it!"

Lena held up her finger and shook it, which made Galen laugh.

"But—" Allie tried to protest.

"Don't make me bring out my brother voice on you!"

Lois came up behind her. "Go ahead, dear. I'll go with her."

"Uh, I don't think so! You need to be here for Allie."

Rebecca climbed into the ambulance while everyone was arguing. "You guys keep arguing. Eli and Hunter are already on their way. We will text you."

With that, the doors closed and off they went.

William just smiled at Lois. "My son is one lucky man. That girl is full of sugar and spice. I like her!" Lois just smiled.

Back at the hospital, Lena was all calmed down and feeling silly like she always did after an attack.

"Hi, Lena." Ironically, Dr. Pizano was the ER doctor that day.

"Dr. Pizano! Oh, I'm so glad it's you."

Dr. Pizano smiled. "Me too."

Dr. Pizano took out some papers and looked them over. Lena was obviously uncomfortable with the look on Dr. Pizano's face. She started to ramble. "Doctor, my asthma attacks are getting worse. I have no problem staying out in the heat usually!"

Just then, Dr. Pizano started smiling. "Well, Lena? Were you feeling lightheaded? Nauseous? Before this particular attack?"

Lena's eyes bugged out of her head. "Yes. What can I do?"

Dr. Pizano smiled at Eli, then Lena. Then, Dr. Pizano wore a stoic look. "Lena, I'm afraid there's nothing you can do in your condition at the moment."

Lena looked horrified. "My condition?"

"Yes, dear. For the rest of summer, you need to avoid the heat. For six months after that, you are going to have to avoid things that trigger your asthma attacks."

Lena did the math in her head. "Dr. Pizano, that's nine months! Do you know how hard it will be to do that?"

Eli started to laugh at Lena's inability to pick up the doctor's clues. He looked at the doctor. "She'll probably have to stay off horses."

Lena just looked at Eli. "What! You can't be serious! For nine—"

Suddenly, a huge smile spread across Lena's face. "Oh … Eli. Nine months. *Do you know what happens in nine months?*"

Eli just smiled. "Well, there's baseball season … hunting season …"

Lena just guffawed at him. "Baseball. Hunting? Eli! Dr. Pizano. Am I having … a baby?" Lena whispered the word. She was afraid to say it.

Dr. Pizano just smiled. "I'm so happy to give you good news, Lena! Yes, you are pregnant. Healthy and pregnant. Now, you'll follow orders?"

Lena started to cry tears of joy. "Yes!"

Eli chuckled. "I think we've tortured her enough. Is she free to go home?"

Dr. Pizano touched her on the shoulder. "She is. Eli, make sure she follows orders."

Eli laughed devilishly. "Oh, don't you worry. She *will* be following orders."

Eli returned Lena to the party as Rebecca and Hunter returned. They all agreed not to say anything until tomorrow because this was Allie's day. Lena felt like she would burst with excitement!

CHAPTER 42

Everyone thought Lena was crazy for waiting seven months to get married. It took a lot of adjustments to her dress, but she wanted to be married before the baby came, yet she wanted to savor the most important day of her life. She still looked stunning, baby bump and all.

Her sisters and Catherine all rushed in and started to gush over the blushing bride, forcing Lena to tears. Rebecca, always the voice of reason, chided her. "Keep those hormones in check, girl! It took hours at that stylist for us all to look like this!"

Avoiding the awkward decision to choose between her sisters, Lena had invoked Rebecca as her maid of honor. Of course, Rebecca looked like she stepped right out of an issue of *Vogue*.

Everyone looked beautiful in gold, Lena's chosen wedding color. Although yellow was her favorite color, she thought gold was more appropriate for a December wedding.

Lois walked in, wearing a nostalgic grin. "Might I have a few moments?" The girls all smiled and obeyed.

"Mama, you look beautiful."

Lois waved her hand. "Hush, child. My days of beauty are over. Yours are just beginning. May I?" She picked up Lena's veil.

"Please do, Mama."

Lena's hair was done in a long wrap down her back, loosely woven with yellow berries. The veil fit nicely to the top of the hair wrap.

"There. As if you could be any more beautiful."

Lena hugged her mother.

"I have something for you. To wrap around your bouquet." Lois pulled out Daddy's favorite blue handkerchief.

"Oh, Mama! You saved it!"

The handkerchief, Daddy's favorite, was worn, tattered, and embroidered with the letters LTM. *Lorenzo Tomas Maleno.* So many times, Lena had used that handkerchief to dry her eyes as a child.

Lois looked at Lena lovingly. "It's blue and incredibly old. Do you know the story behind this thing?" Lois ran her thumb across the loosened embroidery.

Lena put her hand on the handkerchief and stroked the letters that she remembered from so long ago. "No. I just remember using it so many times."

Lois cleared her throat. "Our first Christmas, your daddy bought this ranch, taking every cent we had. All I had for him that Christmas was a box of these handkerchiefs. I embroidered them myself. He wore the others out over the years, but this one he saved. It's yours now."

Lois dried a tear from Lena's cheek with the handkerchief before continuing, which only made her tear up more. "And now I have something for you to borrow." She opened a box to find her great grandma's pearl necklace. Lena tried to protest. "Oh, Mama. I couldn't—"

Lois protested as well. "You will insult me if you don't! Just return them. I know I'm not Hunter's real mother, but he is right. Your dad would have taken him as his own, had he known. I want Rebecca to wear these on her wedding day if it's okay with all of you."

Lena now remembered that Allie had them on as well. "Oh, Mama. It's more than fine with me."

"What about my something new?"

After hearing a knock at the door, William walked inside after Lois said it was okay.

Lois started to leave when William asked her to stay. "Lena, I know things did not come about the right way, with my being your biological father and all. But I'm so glad you had someone that was ready to be a great dad to you when my life was such a mess."

Lena tried to protest, but William stopped her. "No, Lena, you have to let me get through this or I won't say all of it." Lena just sat and put her hands on her lap.

"I would never want to replace Ren. But I thought maybe you'd accept this as your first gift from me?"

Lena opened the box. Inside were a pair of beautiful pearl earrings.

"Oh, William. They are beautiful. Thank you!" Lena looked at her mother in silent conversation, who nodded in approval. "William?"

William looked up from his embarrassment. "Yes?"

"Um, maybe you *and* Mama would like to walk me down the aisle today?"

It was William who was teary now. He looked at Lois, who nodded in approval once more. "I would really love that."

A small knock on the door from Rebecca announced that it was time for them to begin. William and Lois walked Lena down the aisle, but Eli did not take notice. All he saw was the love of his life, looking like an angel walking toward him.

He thought he could even see a halo of light around her. She was the most beautiful thing he had ever seen.

The vows went splendidly, however, the moment Lena was to say 'I do' was a bit more dramatic than she wished.

"I dooooooo … oooohhhhhhh …"

Eli had that panicked look on his face again. "Lena?"

With a look of pain and holding her belly, she looked at the preacher. "Keep going … faster, please …"

Panic-stricken, the minister sped up, quickly pronouncing them husband and wife as Lena felt another kick. "Oooohhhhhhh … Ellllliiiiiii …"

Rebecca went into action again. "Oh boy! Sounds like we are having a baby today!"

Lena was sweating as she tilted her head to look at Rebecca. "Too early …"

Rebecca laughed. "Not according to baby! Let's go!"

Galen snapped into his usual role. "Uh, all of you, please proceed to the reception. Eat our food. We will keep you updated!"

Everyone rushed to the hospital and Hunter insisted on driving Eli. After the last medical emergency, he thought it best for someone to drive him.

Lena had been in labor for about two hours when Eli burst through the doors and into the crowded waiting room. "*It's a boy! I have a boy! I'm a dad!*"

Allie spoke up through everyone's cheers. "Is everyone okay?" The cheers became instantly quiet.

The doctor came in. "He's a little underweight and a little jaundiced, but he's otherwise healthy. He's going to be in the NICU for a little while until he gains a bit of weight and his color returns to normal, but so far, we don't see anything to fear.

I'm going to give Eli and Lena a few minutes, then I'll allow all of you to come in."

Eli went back into the room where Lena was holding their baby. Eli had never seen anything so beautiful in his entire life. He knelt and kissed Lena on the forehead. "I never thought I could love you more than I did. I love you more than I did yesterday. How is that possible?"

Lena looked up and kissed him. "What will we name him?"

Eli put a hand on the baby's little head. "How about Isaiah Robert?"

Lena looked down at her baby. "Eli, I love that name! Where did you get it?"

Eli looked up to heaven. "It was my grandfather's name."

Lena kissed him on the cheek. "What do you say, Isaiah Robert? Do you like it?" Isaiah cooed in his mother's arms. "I think he likes it!"

It was the happiest day of Eli and Helena Miller's lives. They just couldn't imagine it getting any better than this.